"Marco al
way," Lucia t

'Not always,' he said in a husky voice.

'No?' The word squeaked out, betraying her agitation, although Paige was sure he could also hear her erratic heartbeat and feel the nerves jumping in her skin.

'No!' he whispered. 'Because right now Marco has an almost uncontrollable urge to kiss your lips—to see if they taste as sweet as they look. Of course, he would pretend it was a thank-you for caring for his sister Lucia—a casual salute. But he was brought up to treat a woman with respect so he won't do it, but it's proof—no? Proof that Marco doesn't always get his way.'

As she lists her hobbies as reading, reading and reading, it's hardly surprising that **Meredith Webber** fell into writing when she needed a job she could do at home. Not that anyone in the family considers it a 'real job'! She is fortunate enough to live on the Gold Coast in Queensland, Australia, as this gives her the opportunity to catch up with many other people with the same 'unreal' job when they visit the popular tourist area.

Recent titles by the same author:

A HUGS-AND-KISSES FAMILY
HEART-THROB
ONE OF THE FAMILY
MIRACLES AND MARRIAGE
WEDDING AT GOLD CREEK

AN ENTICING PROPOSAL

BY
MEREDITH WEBBER

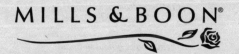

All the characters in this book have no existence outside the imagination of the author, and have no relation whatsoever to anyone bearing the same name or names. They are not even distantly inspired by any individual known or unknown to the author, and all the incidents are pure invention.

First published in Great Britain 2000
Harlequin Mills & Boon Limited,
Eton House, 18-24 Paradise Road, Richmond, Surrey TW9 1SR

© Meredith Webber 2000

ISBN 0 263 82226 5

Set in Times Roman 10½ on 12 pt.
03-0003-51352

Printed and bound in Spain
by Litografia Rosés, S.A., Barcelona

CHAPTER ONE

'I CAN arrange for Dougal to see Dr Barclay this afternoon, Mrs Dean, but I know he won't prescribe antibiotics for Dougal's cold so it would be a waste of your time, coming back again.'

Paige sighed inwardly, wondering why she bothered to waste breath in an argument she was certain to lose.

'All I want is some more of the pink medicine,' Mrs Dean whined. 'Dr Graham let me have some and it fixed Darryl's nose so why can't I have the same for Dougal?'

Forcing back the urge to scream and rant and rave at the woman, Paige explained, for the fourth time in ten minutes, the difference between sinusitis and the common cold, pointed out that the viruses causing the cold would be unaffected by the pink medicine and tried to convince Mrs Dean that rest and a diet including plenty of fluids would soon have young Dougal on the mend.

Young Dougal in the meantime, bored with the conversation, had hooked his thumbs into the corners of his mouth, set his forefingers against his temples and was now contorting his face into various gargoyle shapes which he directed at Paige. If anything, she decided as she listened to Mrs Dean's praise for pink medicine, it improved the looks of a child with a white pudgy face and small raisin eyes, liberally decorated at the moment with the inevitable nasal effusion of the so-called 'common' cold.

A commotion in the waiting room beyond her door suggested restlessness among the natives, so she turned her attention from Dougal's antics and tried once again to prevent an incursion into Ken Barclay's freely given but limited time.

'Look, Mrs Dean, you can ask Carole if Dr Barclay has an appointment available this afternoon, but, believe me, Dougal's cold will run its course and he's better off without unnecessary antibiotics.'

The 'noises off', as script writers might describe the raised voices outside, were increasing so Paige, with a final smile of appreciation for Dougal's facial contortions, stood up to show the visit was at an end. Mrs Dean took the hint, rising laboriously to her feet, grumbling under her breath about no-good nurses and services that were supposed to help the needy, not send them away empty handed.

Having heard it all before, Paige ignored the barbed comments, holding out her hand to offer support to the hugely pregnant woman, wondering idly what the Deans would call the new baby, should it be a girl. Darlene? Dorothy? Diana? After Darryl, Denzil, David, Dennis and Dougal, maybe they would change the initial letter.

'And by the sound of things you've got men in the place.' The grumbling became audible and Paige realised her patient was right. There was at least one man in the waiting room—and not a very happy man at that, if his tone of voice was any indication.

'Supposed to be for women, Tuesdays!' Mrs Dean griped, resisting Paige's attempts to hustle her out the door and calmly rearranging multitudinous layers of clothes around her bulk.

Paige opened the door, more anxious now to discover what was going on than to be free of Mrs Dean. The waiting room was in its usual state of chaos. Children crawled around the floor or fought over the small collection of toys and books she'd managed to accumulate. Their mothers sat on hard plastic chairs, exchanging news and gossip in a desultory fashion, their attention focussed on the confrontation taking place at the reception desk. Some were waiting to see her, but others would have appointments with Sue Chalmers, an occupational therapist who volunteered her time on Tuesday mornings to run a small toy library.

Carole Benn, the community service's receptionist, was in place behind the high counter, which provided her with little protection from the man who was leaning across it, waggling his finger in her face and growling threateningly at her.

A second man stood slightly behind this aggressive type, looking remote and disinterested, seemingly oblivious to the noise and activity all around him. His colour was bad—olive overlaid with grey. An illness perhaps. Had the pair strayed in here, thinking it was a medical practice? She studied the silent man covertly—from a female not a nursing point of view this time. Bad colour did little to diminish the magnetism of a face which could have been carved from mountain rock—like the heads of presidents somewhere in the United States.

The wayward thought flitted through Paige's mind as she ushered Mrs Dean towards the counter and raised her eyebrows at Carole. Carole lifted one hand and made an almost imperceptible shooing movement with her fingers but the irate man observed the motion and spun immediately towards Paige.

'So you are Paige Morgan!' he said in accusatory tones. 'This woman tries to tell me you are not available. I am Benelli and this is Prince Alessandro Francesco Marcus Alberici.'

To the astonishment of Paige, and all the occupants of

the waiting room, the younger man came to attention and all but clicked his heels together as he indicated the second man with a wild flourish of one hand and a movement of his body that suggested obeisance.

'Ah, at last my prince has come.' Paige clasped her hands theatrically in front of her chest and raised her eyes to the ceiling. Then she grinned at Carole. 'Wouldn't you know he'd arrive on a Tuesday when I'm too busy for a coronation.'

Inside, she wasn't quite so light-hearted as bits of her fizzed and squished in a most unseemly manner—the result of another quick appraisal of the second man's bone structure.

Lust at first sight?

With a determined effort, she turned away, concentrating on the underling, hoping to surprise a smile in his eyes, some confirmation he wasn't serious.

'Am I supposed to guess something—or answer a question and get a prize?' she hazarded. 'Is it a joke of some kind, or a new form of fund-raising? I'm afraid my sense of humour's a bit dulled this morning and, as for money, this place takes every penny I can scrounge up.'

Mr Benelli turned an unattractive shade of puce—now she had two bad-complexioned strangers in her waiting room! He jumped up and down—or rose on his toes to give that impression—and began waggling his forefinger at her.

'This is no joke! He is a prince, a real prince, and he does not want money.'

'Well, that's a change,' Paige replied, risking a swift glance towards the 'real prince' and catching what appeared to be a glint of humour in his black eyes. Black eyes? Did eyes come in black? Not that she could see them closely enough to judge eye colour accurately. 'What *does* he want?'

She shook her head as she heard her own question. Why the hell was she carrying on this conversation through an intermediary?

'He wishes to speak with you on a matter of extreme urgency,' Mr Benelli informed her, and for the first time Paige caught the hint of a foreign accent in his properly worded and pronounced English and realised that he, too, had the dark hair and olive complexion of his companion, a colouring she associated with Mediterranean origins.

Surely it couldn't be... Her heart skittered at the half-formed thought.

'I'll be free at twelve,' she said crisply, hoping her rising anxiety wasn't apparent in the words. 'Perhaps you could both come back then.' She glanced again towards the second man, realised the grey colour was probably fatigue and added, 'Or you could wait here if you prefer.'

The offer failed to please Benelli, who all but exploded on the spot as he poured out his indignation.

'This is urgent, he must see you now. The car waits outside to drive him back to Sydney. He is busy man. Important. Not to be—'

Paige missed the end of the sentence, too intent on trying to settle the new upheaval within her—one that had nothing to do with lust. Perhaps it *was* a joke, she hoped desperately. Hadn't she glimpsed a gleam of humour in the dark eyes? And why didn't the second man speak if it was his errand—his urgency?

He answered the second question almost as she thought it.

'We will wait, Benelli,' he said, in a voice that vibrated across Paige's skin like a bow drawn across violin strings.

Shivering at the effect, she pulled a file from the holder on her office door and called the name of the next patient, seeing Benelli offer the newly vacated chair to the 'prince', the man refusing it and propping himself on the window-ledge as her father had done during her childhood when this had been their living room, not a place for those who could not afford other services to wait—and hope.

Her father had been a tall man—a little over six feet—and the window-ledge had been comfortable for him. But she'd never found it anything but awkward to perch there, although at five feet eight she wasn't a short woman.

And why you're thinking about how tall you are is beyond me, she admonished herself silently, leading Mabel Kruger into the room, then closing the door firmly on the unwelcome visitors.

''Andsome enough to be a prince,' Mabel remarked, settling into the visitor's chair and lifting her leg onto the stool Paige had pulled towards her.

'Why should we expect princes to be handsomer than ordinary mortals?' she asked crossly, peeling dressings off Mabel's ulcer as gently and carefully as she could.

'They are in books,' Mabel pointed out. 'And, apart from that Charles, the Queen's lads are good-looking.'

'Well, I'm sure she'd be pleased to hear you say so,' Paige responded, talking to distract Mabel's attention as she debrided dead tissue, cleaning out the gaping hole and wondering if a skin graft might eventually be necessary or if they were winning the battle against infection. 'Though I think I prefer blond men. Why are princes always depicted as dark?'

They chatted on, and she knew she was diverting herself as well as Mabel. Not wanting to think about the phone call she'd made, about betrayal—and being caught out. No, the two couldn't be connected. A simple phone call in return was all she'd expected—wanted.

So why did she feel sick with apprehension? Why was she harbouring a grim foreknowledge that the strangers in her waiting room were connected with Lucia?

She set aside unanswerable questions. Mabel was explaining, with minimal use of the letter 'h', about the beauty of the princes she'd encountered in the fairytale books of her youth. She then moved on to wonder about the reliability or otherwise of princes, given the unreliability of men in general. Paige let her talk and concentrated all her attention on her task, peeling the protective backing off the new dressing, then pressing it firmly in place.

'Now, leave it there all week unless your leg swells or you notice any unusual redness or feel extra pain,' she told her patient. 'And rest with your leg up whenever you can—'

'So I don't 'ave to go to 'ospital and get a graft!'

Mabel repeated the usual ending to this warning, then she patted Paige—who was still kneeling on the floor, pulling Mabel's sock up over the dressing—on the head and said, 'Not that you don't deserve a prince, girl.'

Paige looked up at her and smiled.

'Don't wish that on me. I don't want any man—let alone a princely one,' she teased, using the back of Mabel's chair to lever herself up to her feet.

'You mightn't want one,' Mabel argued, 'but you're the kind of girl as needs a man about the place—well, not needs, maybe, but should 'ave. I see your eyes when you look at those kids sometimes, and the babies. That fancy doctor did you no favour, getting you all interested in things like marriage then taking off with that floozy.'

Well, that's a different take on my break-up with

James, Paige thought as she helped Mabel to her feet. Was that how all her patients viewed the nine-day wonder of it all? How her friends saw it?

'Not all men are the same,' Mabel declared with as much authority as if she'd made that notable discovery herself.

Paige grinned at the pronouncement. She walked the elderly woman to the door and saw her out, her eyes going immediately to the man framed in the window embrasure. No, all men were not the same, she admitted silently, then trembled as if a draught had brushed across her neck.

Calling for the next patient, she turned back inside so she didn't have to look at the stranger in their midst.

Well, you mightn't have to look at him, but you'll have to think about him some time soon, she reminded herself, grabbing the chubby two-year-old who'd scampered through the door ahead of her mother, intent on climbing onto Paige's desk and creating as much havoc as she could.

'Not today, Josephine,' she murmured as she swung the child into her arms and gave her a quick hug. 'Is she any calmer on the Effilix?' she asked, turning to the young woman who'd followed them into the room and settled into the chair with a tired sigh.

Yes, she had more to worry about than princes—or men either—at the moment, she reminded herself, watching Debbie and wondering how she juggled her studies and motherhood.

'I suppose it depends on your definition of calmer,' Debbie Palmer replied with a wry grin that told Paige no miracle cure had been effected by the natural therapy. 'But Susie's been giving her massages every second day and that seems to have a good effect on her, and the other mothers at playgroup feel she's interacting much better with their kids.'

'Well, that's something,' Paige said in her most encouraging voice, setting Josie back on her feet and handing her a small bright top, demonstrating how it spun, then watching as the little hands tried to duplicate the action. In her opinion, Josephine was a very bright child with an active, enquiring mind, but too many people had muttered 'hyperactive' to Debbie, and the young single mother now feared a diagnosis of ADD—the attention deficit disorder—which was the popular label for behavioural problems used among parents and school teachers at the moment.

Debbie was ambivalent about the drugs used to treat the disorder—some days determined to keep Josie off medication, while on others wanting the relief she imagined they might bring. Paige had come down on the side of a drug-free life for the child and pressed this point of view whenever possible, although at times she wondered how she would feel in a similar situation.

'I've arranged for a paediatrician to see Josie next month,' she said. 'It's a Dr Kerr, and he's agreed to meet you here so she's in familiar territory. But as I've said before, Deb, there's no guarantee he'll come up with anything. It's very difficult to pin a label on so young a child.'

Debbie looked at her without answering, then she shrugged and grinned.

'Seems a little unfair, doesn't it? You get a prince and I get a paediatrician!'

'I can't imagine he's really a prince,' Paige retorted. 'And, even if he is, what would I want with one?'

'Well, he's decorative for a start,' Debbie pointed out. 'And he oozes that magnetic kind of sex appeal only some men have, in case you're too old to remember what sex appeal is.'

Paige chuckled in spite of the worry Debbie's conversation had regenerated.

'Am I walking around looking jaded and depressed? Or like someone gnawing at her bones with frustration?' she said. 'Mabel's just told me I need a man and now you're here offering me good-looking sex.'

'Oh, he's beyond good-looking,' Debbie argued, taking the top from her daughter before it could be hurled across the room. She leaned forward and demonstrated its action once more, then smiled as she watched the little figure squat down on the floor and try again.

Paige watched the interaction of mother and child, saw Debbie's smile, so full of love for this difficult little mortal she'd conceived by accident, and felt the tug of envious longing which told her Mabel was right.

But the prince, if prince he was and her assumptions were correct, had come to reclaim his wife, not carry a tired community nurse off into some fabled distance on his shining white charger.

She sighed.

'Sighing's usually my line, not yours,' Debbie told her. 'Are you OK?'

'A bit tired,' Paige explained, not untruthfully. The problem of what to do with her uninvited house guest had been keeping her awake at night for the last month.

'That's why you need a change—a holiday,' Debbie reminded her. 'You've been working for what...four years without a break. You deserve a bit of time to yourself.'

To do what? Paige thought, but she didn't say it. She *did* need a break, needed to get right away somewhere so she wouldn't be tempted to step in if things went wrong at the service, answer calls at night which some-one else should take.

But with Lucia?

She sighed again.

'OK, OK, I get the message,' Debbie said. 'I won't keep you. I brought back the library toys and Sue chose some new ones for Josie, so all I need is a time for Dr Kerr's appointment and I'm out of here.' She grinned cheekily at Paige. 'Leaving you with only one patient to go before the prince!'

'Lucky me! Who is it? Do you know?'

'I think it's Mrs Epstein. I noticed her in the corner, huddling into that black wool coat of hers and trying to look invisible.'

'Poor thing. She's not at all well, and hasn't had a proper medical check since Sally Carruthers left town. She refuses to see a male doctor. I guess eventually someone will have to drive her down to Tamworth to see one of the women in practice down there. Would you send her in, to save me going to the door? Just lift her file out of the slot and give it to her to bring in.'

Paige gave Josie a hug and said goodbye to Debbie, then sat down at her desk and buried her head in her hands. One more patient then the prince to confront. He *had* to have come about Lucia, so what did she tell him? She could hardly reveal Lucia's presence in the house without at least consulting her—explaining about the phone call and why she'd made it.

And she couldn't leave this room to go upstairs and talk to Lucia without being seen by her two unwelcome visitors.

Unless…

She glanced towards the windows, stood up and walked across to open the one closer to her desk. To poke her head out and look up. As a child she'd climbed both up and down the Virginia creeper innumerable times, but would it hold an adult's weight?

And was she seriously considering climbing up there?

'Seeking an escape route?'

The deep voice made her spin around, and she knew from the flash of heat in her cheeks that her stupid pale skin was flushing guiltily.

'The room was warm,' she sputtered, compounding her stupidity with the lie. She took control. 'Anyway, I've another patient to see before you.'

'Your patient has departed,' he responded coolly.

'Or been intimidated into leaving by your presence,' Paige retorted, curbing an urge to add a scorching remark about princely arrogance. 'What's happened to your side-kick?'

'Sidekick?' The man looked bemused.

'Mr Benelli. The guy who bowed you in.'

'Ah, you took offence at his behaviour. I can understand that reaction, but to check him, tell him this ceremony was not what I wanted or desired, would have been to humiliate him in front of your patients.'

Paige stared at him, though why his compassion for a fellow man should startle her she didn't know. Unless she'd assumed princes were above such things! Which reminded her—

'Are you really a prince?'

He shrugged, moved further into the room and smiled.

Bad move, that—making him smile. The rearrangement of his features made him even more devastatingly attractive—and, coming closer, it had brought his eyes into view. Not black but darkest blue, almost navy.

'I am Francesco Alberici. The title ''prince'' is a hangover from bygone days—something I do not use myself.

Benelli is an official at our consulate in Sydney. It is he who sees honour in a useless appellation, not myself.'

He'd held out his hand as he'd said his name, and politeness had decreed she take it. But to let it rest in his as he finished speaking? Another mistake.

She took control, stuck her still-warm but nonetheless offending hand into the pocket of her blazer and looked—confidently, she hoped—into his eyes.

'So, now we've cleared up the prince business, how can I help you?'

As if I don't know, an inner voice quailed, and she regretted not escaping through the window, even if she hadn't climbed the creeper.

'You phoned me—left a message.'

Marco watched the colour fluctuate beneath her cheeks—no doubt she was considering what lie to tell him—and wondered about her background. With that pale skin, cornsilk-coloured hair falling in a straight drop to chin level and the smatter of freckles across her nose, she certainly didn't fit his image of a bronzed Australian. But, then, this New England city in the northern tableland area of New South Wales had the feel of an English market town, in spite of the lush sheep country which surrounded it.

'You're Marco?'

Her question, when it came, held surprise—and, he suspected, dread. Or guilt?

'Who else?' he said harshly, surprised to find an inner anger surging into the reply. He could usually control his emotions better than that. Tiredness? The long flight? Or the months of gut-wrenching, muscle-straining, heart-breaking worry over Lucia?

He curbed the anger as wide spaced green eyes, flecked

with the gold of the sunlight outside, stared warily into his.

'Why didn't you phone?'

'I came instead.'

'Why?'

The question gave him momentary pause, then the anger churned again, rising, threatening to erupt.

'To take Lucia home,' he said bluntly.

Paige had seen him stiffen earlier, guessed at anger, saw the tension in his body, controlled now but ready to explode. She wondered about violence. Was that why Lucia had fled? She had to forget her own reaction to the man—that strange and almost instant attraction. Right now she needed to stall, to buy time. With time maybe she could persuade Lucia to talk about her flight, before revealing her whereabouts to anyone. Or this man's presence in town to Lucia!

She tried for innocence in her expression—in her voice.

'Lucia?' she repeated in dulcet tones.

Wrong move! His body language told her she'd unwittingly lit the fuse to set him off. He stepped closer, spoke more softly, but there was no escaping the rage emanating from his body and trembling in his words.

'Yes, Lucia, Miss Morgan. And don't act the innocent with me. You phoned my private work number, a new number only a handful of people know, you asked for Marco—a name only Lucia and my family use to address me. You left a message—said you wanted to speak to me. I haven't come halfway around the world to play games with you, so speak to me, Miss Morgan. Or tell me where she is and let her explain her behaviour.'

Paige shivered under the onslaught of his words—and the emotion accompanying them. No way could she inflict him on her ill and unhappy house guest. But how to tell an enraged husband—however handsome and sexy he might be—you won't let him see his wife, without risking bodily harm to yourself? She gulped in some replenishing air, waited for the oxygen to fire into her blood, then squared up to him.

'I will speak to her, ask her if she wishes to see you.'

'You will...'

Well, at least she'd rendered him speechless!

She raised her hands as if to show helplessness. 'I can't do any more than that.'

He glared at her, his eyes sparkling with the fierceness of his anger.

'Then why did you contact me? To tease me? Torture me even more? Was it her idea? Did she say, "Let's upset Marco in this new way"?'

The agony in his voice pierced through to her heart and she found herself wanting to put her arms around him, comfort him—for all her doubts about his behaviour towards his wife.

'She doesn't know I contacted you,' she said softly—feeling the guilt again. Wondering how to explain.

He was waiting, the fire dying from his eyes, the grey colour taking over again.

'Please, sit down. Do you want a drink—something hot—tea, coffee?'

No reply, but he did slump into the chair. He ran the fingers of his right hand through his dark hair, then stared at her. Still waiting.

'She came to me—off a backpackers' coach. Do you know about backpackers?'

He shrugged and managed to look both disbelieving and affronted at the same time. 'Young tourists travelling on the cheap. But a coach? Lucia? Backpacking? And why would she come here?'

Well, the last question was easy. If you took it literally.

'The bus company has a number of coaches which follow the same route through the country towns of New South Wales. People buy a six-month ticket and can get on and off wherever they like—staying a few days in some places, longer in others. This is a very popular stopping-off place and the company recommends the health service as a number of the professionals here speak more than one language.'

'Parla italiano?'

The words sounded soft and mellifluous in Paige's ears and again she felt a pang of sorrow—a sense of loss for something she'd never had.

'If you're asking if I speak Italian, the answer's no. I used a phrase book to leave a message on your answerphone. I studied Japanese and Indonesian and can get by in German. Many of the European tourists also speak or understand it, so I can communicate to a certain extent.'

'Which is a credit to you but isn't diverting me from the subject of Lucia, Miss Morgan.'

Mellifluous? Steely, more like!

'Or your phone call,' he added, in a no-less-determined voice.

'She wasn't well, and I sensed…'

How to explain her conviction that Lucia was in trouble—ill, lost and vulnerable—so alone that to take her in and care for her had been automatic.

She looked at the man from whom the young woman had fled and wondered how to tell him why she'd been compelled to phone him.

'She wasn't like the usual backpackers I see. Mostly they're competent young people, clued up, able to take care of themselves, if you know what I mean. Lucia struck me as someone so far out of her depth she was in danger of drowning.' She met his eyes now, challenging him yet willing him to understand. 'But I also felt she'd been very much loved and cherished all her life,' she admitted, 'and from the little she told me, I guessed someone, somewhere, would be frantically worried about her whereabouts.'

He said nothing, simply stared at her as if weighing her words, wondering whether to believe them.

'She doesn't know I made that call,' Paige admitted, feeling heat flood her cheeks again. 'I looked through her passport one day and found the number pencilled in the back of it. I felt you—her family—someone some-where—might need to know she was alive.'

He bowed his head, letting his chin rest against his chest, and she saw his chest rise and fall as be breathed deeply.

'Yes,' he said, after a long pause. 'I—we all—did need to know she was alive.'

She studied him. Saw tiredness in the way his body was slumped in the chair. But when he raised his head and looked into her eyes there was no sign of fatigue—and the anger which she'd seen earlier still lit his from within.

'Did she tell you why she ran away?' he demanded.

Paige shrugged.

'She told me very little,' she said bluntly. 'All I've done is guess.'

'Abominable girl!' the man declared, straightening in his chair and flinging his arms into the air in a gesture of frustration. 'She's been spoiled all her life, that's her trouble. Cherished is right! Of course she was cherished. And how does she repay that love and affection? How

does she treat those who love her? By taking off!
Running away! Leaving without a word to anyone, a note
from Rome to her mother, saying she will be all right!
Then nothing for months. We all assume she's dead! *Dio
Madonna!*'

Perhaps it was as well she didn't speak Italian. The
intonation of the words told her it was a phrase unlikely
to be repeatable in polite company. Not that the man
didn't look magnificent in his rage, on his feet now and
prowling the room like a sleek black animal, still muttering foreign imprecations under his breath and moving
his hands as if to conduct his voice. But watching him
perform, that wasn't getting them anywhere, and no matter how magnificent and full of sex appeal he was, he'd
be out of her life by tomorrow so the sooner she got rid
of him now, the sooner she could tackle Lucia.

And the thought of *her* reaction to this latest development wasn't all that appealing! Paige stood, drew herself up to her full height and assumed her most busi-
nesslike expression. The one she used when asking for
government funding from petty officials put on earth to
frustrate her plans for the community centre.

'If you rant and rave at her like that, I can understand
why she ran off,' she said crisply. 'Now, if you tell me
where you're staying, I'll have a talk to her and get back
to you.'

'Staying?' He sounded as shocked as if she'd suggested he strip naked in the main street. 'I am not staying!
I have work to do. I must get back to Italy. I am—in
fact, we, Lucia and I, are booked on a flight out of
Sydney tomorrow morning.'

Paige stared at him in astonishment.

'You flew out from Italy to Australia for a day? You
thought you could arrive here, drive up, wrest Lucia forc-

ibly into the car, then career back down the highway and be out of the country within twenty-four hours?'

Maybe her amazement caught his attention for he stopped his pacing and faced her.

'I did not know where this town was—how far away from the capital,' he said stiffly. 'I gave the telephone number to a person at the embassy. He found the address—this address—and arranged to bring me here. It was not until I was in the car I learned she was at a far-off place—a regional centre I think Benelli called it.' He paused, then added, 'He said it was still possible to be back in Sydney late this evening and make the flight to-morrow.'

As that pause was the first hint of weakness she'd seen in the man—apart from the fatigue—she took it as an opening and pounced.

'Well, I suggest you see Mr Benelli again and ask him to arrange accommodation for you, and rearrange your flight home. Apart from anything else, I doubt Lucia is well enough to travel.'

She watched the colour drain from his face.

'What is wrong with her?' he demanded, and a hoarseness in his voice told her of his love for Lucia.

CHAPTER TWO

How to answer? Tell a man his wife had gestational diabetes mellitus when he didn't know she was pregnant? And Marco wouldn't know because Lucia hadn't known herself—hadn't even guessed what might be wrong with her. The diabetes was an added complication, one not usually occurring until late into the second trimester of pregnancy when the foetus was extracting more nutrients from the maternal source, but the trauma of leaving home could have triggered a possible predisposition to it, bringing it on earlier than usual.

The thoughts rushed through Paige's head and she studied him as she decided what to say. He didn't look like a man who'd give in easily and telling him Lucia was carrying his child, that would hand him an added incentive to force her to return to him. It would also betray Lucia's trust. Again!

Hide behind professional discretion?

She didn't think this man would take too kindly to this ethical solution to her dilemma but what the hell.

'I need to speak to her before I can give you any information about her health or where she's staying,' Paige replied, already feeling the waves of his anger as it built again. 'Give me an hour—or maybe two—and I'll contact you, or, better still, you could phone me here.'

She opened a desk drawer to get a card for him then realised it would show this building as her home address as well as that of the health service. Bring him closer than she wanted at the moment. Pulling out a scrap of paper instead, she jotted down her number and pushed it across the desk.

He was standing opposite her, staring at her with an unnerving intensity.

'I already have your phone number, Miss Morgan,' he said softly. 'What I don't know is Lucia's whereabouts. Now, are you going to tell me where she is or do I call in your police force?'

She did her straightening-up thing again, hoping to look more in control.

'Lucia is an adult—able to make her own decisions. No police force in the world can compel a woman to return to a situation from which she's fled.'

She wasn't absolutely certain about the truth of this statement but he wasn't to know that. Not that he seemed to be taking much notice. In fact he was laughing at her.

Derisively!

'Fled, Miss Morgan? Aren't you overdramatising the situation?'

Damn her cheeks—just when she wanted to appear super-cool they were heating up again.

'You said yourself she ran away,' she countered hotly. 'And now you've arrived, like some vengeful gaoler, to take her back—threatening me with the police force! No, I think if anyone's overdramatising, it's you, Prince Highfaluting-whatever. Sweeping in here, making demands. I'm the one who's being reasonable about this!'

OK, so she didn't sound very reasonable right now, but he'd made her mad. And that superior expression on his carved-rock face made her even madder.

He ignored her rudeness, nodded once, stepped back a pace from his position near the desk and said, 'I will give you an hour, Miss Morgan, but that is all. For some reason you are under the impression Lucia will not wish to see me. You are wrong. She will be glad and grateful that I have arrived to take care of her.'

'Oh yeah?' Paige muttered with as much cynicism as she could muster, though why his sudden switch to politeness was aggravating her more than his anger had she didn't know. 'Well, we'll let her be the judge of that. Will you phone?'

His eyes scanned her face, as if he wanted to imprint it on his mind, and when he finally replied—saying, 'No, I will return to this house,'—Paige felt a tremor of apprehension flutter down her spine.

And dealing with Lucia wasn't any easier. When Paige confessed she'd found the number in the passport and had phoned it, her guest had pouted and turned her face to the wall, prepared to sulk.

'I had to let someone know you were alive,' Paige said desperately. 'It wasn't fair that all your friends and family should have been worrying themselves to death—imagining the worst of fates for you. I just didn't expect him to come.'

The slim figure shot upright, delight and apprehension illuminating her usually pale face, giving her a radiant beauty.

'He's here? Marco's here? Oh, why did you not tell me straight away? Where is he? Bring him to me! Now, Paige, now!'

One of the few things she had told Paige was that she'd only been married two months before she'd left. It hadn't taken her long to learn imperious ways!

'Are you sure you want to see him?' Paige asked, mistrusting this swift change of mood. 'He's here to take you home.'

The beauty faded, leaving her visitor pale again.

'Of course! He *would* have come for that reason. Trust

him to do such a thing, thinking he would persuade me.' She pouted again, then tossed the cloud of soft dark hair and added defiantly, 'Well, I won't go!'

There was another pause, and Paige could almost read the expressions that washed across Lucia's face—hope, longing, doubt and confusion.

'But I'd like to see Marco,' Lucia continued tremulously. 'Will you stay with me while he visits? Not let him bully me or talk me into going home?'

Paige sighed. The very last thing she wanted to do was play gooseberry between a man and his wife—particularly, for some reason, between the man in question and this young woman she'd come to like.

'I think you should talk to him on your own,' she said. 'Don't you think you owe him that?'

Huge brown eyes gazed piteously into hers.

'But he'll talk me into going back,' Lucia wailed. 'Into doing whatever he wants. Marco *always* gets his way.'

I can believe that, Paige thought, picturing the man who'd invaded her office, but the idea of acting as a chaperone at this forthcoming meeting was making her feel quite ill. She patted Lucia's arm and suggested she get up and have a shower before her visitor arrived.

'I don't know about staying with you while you talk to him, but I'll be right outside the door if you need me.' She watched Lucia stand and saw her slender frame silhouetted against the light from the window, a neat bulge showing the eighteenth week of her pregnancy but still far too thin to be healthy, and another idea occurred to her.

'If he does want to take you home and you decide you'd prefer to stay, we can use your health as an excuse. In my opinion, you're not yet stable enough, even on the

insulin, to be undertaking an arduous flight and I'm sure
your obstetrician would agree with me.'

From the new expressions on Lucia's face, this suggestion was receiving a mixed reception. Paige came
closer and put her arms around the woman's narrow
shoulders.

'You're not happy here,' she said gently. 'Are you sure
you wouldn't be better off at home? Perhaps not with
your husband, but with family or friends? People you
know and love? People who would care for you?'

Lucia shrugged away from her.

'My family would say my place is with my husband,'
she said bitterly. 'I can hear them now. My mother especially—and my sisters. It was their idea I marry, their
fault, all of this.'

Paige hesitated. Lucia was emotional, but the words
had more petulance than fear and, thinking of the handsome man with the dark blue eyes—remembering his
genuine pain when he'd talked of Lucia's flight—she
pressed a little further.

'Didn't you want the marriage? Did you love someone
else?'

Lucia shook her head and began to cry, silent tears
sliding down her cheeks.

'Love someone else?' She sobbed out the words. 'How
could I when he was all I knew, the man I was destined
to marry? I loved him, and only him—but he... He had
different ideas about love—ideas Italian men of position
held many centuries ago, not now, although I know many
men cheat on their wives. When I told him I would not
allow it, he laughed and said he would take a mistress if
he wished for who was I to stop him?' She sniffed, then
finished with a tilt of her head, 'So I ran away!'

Paige stared at her, unable to believe what she was

hearing. Well, she could believe the arrogant man she'd met downstairs might have such antediluvian views, but that a vague and possibly teasing threat about some future indiscretion had made Lucia flee? She'd imagined assault—either physical or emotional—shuddered over her mental images of what the gentle, trusting soul might have endured. But to run away because he'd said he might take a mistress one day?

'Go take a shower and get dressed,' she said abruptly. 'And while you're in there make up your mind whether you want to see him or not. I'll have lunch ready when you come out, then you'll have time to see him before we do the next blood glucose test.'

Lucia grimaced but she left the sunny sitting room where she spent most of each day—lying on the couch watching soaps on TV—and turned towards the bathroom. Paige watched her go and wondered, not for the first time, what on earth had prompted her to take the girl-woman in.

Instinct.

Ironic that the same inbuilt warning system had sent up flares when she'd first seen Lucia's husband! Only then they'd signalled 'danger' instead of 'help'.

'I will see him,' Lucia announced when she returned, dressed in loose-fitting tan trousers and a golden yellow mohair sweater—looking stunning for all her poor health. 'I will see him here and tell him I cannot go home.'

Paige sighed but didn't argue, going downstairs to the kitchen and fixing a sandwich for the two of them, counting off the calories in Lucia's meal and writing them down so she knew how many her patient-guest had eaten. In the beginning she'd tried to persuade Lucia to undertake this task for herself, but had finally given up, deciding it was more important to teach her to do her own injections and blood glucose tests.

Huh!

'OK, your turn to do the injection.' She said this every time and every time Lucia came up with some excuse for not taking the responsibility. Paige fitted a needle to the syringe, lifted the insulin out of the refrigerator and set it on the table. 'Just try filling the syringe, Lucia. Pull down to the mark, stick the needle through the rubber top on the bottle and press the plunger in to release the air.'

'I cannot touch that needle, I might injure myself!'

It was the usual argument—one they had four times a day—so both knew their part in it.

'You can't injure yourself if you hold it properly. Do you want to be dependent on someone else all through your pregnancy?' Paige grinned to herself as she realised why this argument had had little effect on Lucia in the past. Given the princely husband, the younger woman had probably had swarms of servants catering to her every whim—being dependent on someone was a habit rather than a concern.

'You do it, Paige, just today?'

The voice cajoled and the brown eyes begged.

Paige grumbled about her weakness in always giving in, and filled the syringe with the fast-acting insulin Lucia would need for her body to handle the meal she was about to eat.

'But I'm not staying with you while you talk to him,' Paige warned, determined to win one argument today. 'You've got to see him on your own.'

Lucia didn't argue. In fact, she smiled and looked excited, flushed with a soft and youthful radiance which made Paige feel older than her twenty-five years and unaccountably depressed as she tackled her own lunch with far less gusto than her guest.

And the depression wasn't lifted by the stern expression on her next visitor's face. She had sent Lucia upstairs to the sitting room and was waiting outside the house when the long black car with the consular plates drew up. Although the autumn sun was warm, she found herself shivering as he alighted. A fact that didn't escape him.

'You should be wearing a jacket,' he chided, and moved towards her as if to wrap his arm around her shoulders. The cold was replaced by warmth and she dodged ahead, leading him towards the side door which led directly into her flat.

'No wonder she ran away,' she muttered, more to herself than him. 'If you tell a *stranger* what to wear…'

'Pardon?'

'It was nothing.' She reached the door and paused, then turned to face him, looking into his eyes—hoping to read his reaction to what she had to say. 'Lucia has agreed to see you, but I'd like to say…' The words petered out under the intensity of that blue gaze. Pull yourself together! Think of Lucia, not eyes that seem to drill into your soul. 'She's in a very fragile state, easily upset, both physically and emotionally. Will you remember that? Treat her gently?'

Or eyes that darken dangerously!

'And what do you imagine I intend to do to her? Throw her over my shoulder and force her to return with me? Is that how an Australian man would behave, Miss Morgan? How you would like a man to act with you?'

Damn him—and her give-away cheeks! The image had made her go hot all over. Battling to regain control, she tried an imperious look of her own.

'Australia has as many gentlemen as any other country, though they may not carry fancy titles, and, no, I wouldn't expect any man to ride roughshod over a woman, but men can exert more than physical power.'

'And women can't?' he countered, fixing her with a look so quizzical she wondered how she'd come to be arguing with him.

'Just treat her gently,' Paige said, turning abruptly away before her face betrayed even more of her inner chaos. She'd never felt such a physical reaction to another human being. For the first time in her life, she was beginning to understand what people meant when they talked about instant attraction. And sex appeal! Not only could she now accept its existence, but she had to acknowledge that this man had it by the bucket-load.

Yet his wife had run away from him.

The thought occurred to her as she walked up the stairs ahead of him, hearing his firm tread behind her, feeling his presence in the nerves down her spine, aware even of a faint whiff of some sophisticated cologne or aftershave—not a pungent or overpowering odour, but more a tantalising hint of something smooth and sleek but very masculine.

Help! Now it seemed her thoughts were doing the running away—straight into a fantasy land.

'Lucia is inside.'

She knocked and was about to grasp the doorknob when the door flew open and a vision of loveliness in a bright mohair sweater flung herself into the waiting arms of the prince.

Which is how all good fairytales should end, Paige reminded herself as she returned to the kitchen to play Cinderella-before-the-ball, washing the lunch dishes, working out a dinner menu, wondering what she could do about arranging nutritious meals for Lucia to take on the plane if her prince insisted she return home immediately.

By the time footsteps sounded on the stairs, she'd not only organised what they'd have for dinner but had cleaned the kitchen thoroughly, written out a shopping list, contemplated polishing the silver and settled for washing the floor instead—anything to keep her mind off what might be happening upstairs.

And, no, she wouldn't take that thought any further either!

She straightened up as the heavy footfall hesitated only fractionally at the bottom of the steps then turned unerringly towards the kitchen. One glance at the dark scowl on Marco's face told her the reunion hadn't gone quite the way he'd planned.

'Lucia tells me you will explain her medical condition. She pleaded tiredness, a need to rest and, in fact, she does not look well. Is this a new game of hers or is she indeed ill?'

Paige felt the words jar against her brain.

'She didn't tell you?'

The scowl deepened.

'Tell me what?'

Drat the girl? What was Paige supposed to do? Blurt out to the man that his wife was not only pregnant but suffering a complication which required a strict medical and personal regimen of care?

Marco watched the slim, pale-skinned woman pace up and down beside the kitchen table, leaving a trail of shoe prints on the floor she'd evidently just washed, and wondered what he'd said to cause so much agitation. Not that having Lucia as a house guest wasn't enough to drive anyone to distraction. Spoilt, that's what she was.

But this woman had seemed so sensible—so 'together'
as he'd heard it described in English. And she'd taken
Lucia in and cared for her, been kind enough to feel
concern for her relatives—something which still wasn't
worrying Lucia over-much.

'If you prefer to walk and talk, I would be glad to be
outside for a while. I was cooped up in the plane, then
the car journey and a hotel.'

She glanced up at him, as if surprised to hear his voice.
Had she forgotten he was there—that he was waiting for
an answer? Now she looked at her watch and frowned as
if calculating something. How much time she could waste
perhaps? How long she could procrastinate?

'Actually, I have to be outside fairly soon anyway. I
have some house calls to make, and as they're close I
usually walk.' She smiled at him, and he caught an echo
of it in her eyes and knew he'd misjudged the frown.
That was a real smile, not the plastic version most women
he knew could flash at will—trained by years of practice
at society functions where a camera could catch any unwary facial grimace and reveal it in the daily papers.

He found himself hoping she'd smile some more during the short time they would have together.

'I will walk with you,' he announced, and saw her
frown again, sigh, then shrug her shoulders as if she
wasn't happy about his presence but would accept it.

'Most women would be happy to walk with me,' he
growled, riled by the reaction, but she appeared not to
have heard his piqued comment. She slipped past him to
the door, turning to say, 'I'd better check on Lucia before
we go.' Then she disappeared into the passageway.

It was because he was tired that her patent lack of
interest in him niggled. Although he'd had his share of
attractive women as friends and lovers, he certainly

didn't expect every woman he met to fall at his feet. He glared at the empty doorway, then realised the futility of such an act and chuckled, turning his attention instead to the room where he waited.

It was attractive in a homely way—a big practical kitchen with tiled floors and stained timber cupboards and benches. A long wooden table was scarred by use, and the two comfortable armchairs pulled up close to the fuel stove hinted that this room was the real heart of the dwelling. It seemed to hold the faint echoes of happy family gatherings and the accumulated aroma of good hearty meals. Almost an Italian kitchen in its ambience, he decided, sniffing the air and touching the leaves of the herbs which flourished in pots along the windowsill.

Did this flat at the back of the health service come with Miss Morgan's job? Did she live here alone—when she wasn't bringing home stray runaways like Lucia?

He felt the now-familiar clutch of fear Lucia's disappearance had caused, then said a silent prayer of thanks that she had fallen into such safe and apparently sensible hands.

'OK, let's go!'

The soft, slightly husky voice summoned him from the doorway. She'd pulled a padded jacket over her cream sweater and trousers and the dark green colour deepened the colour in her eyes, making them more green than gold. He'd read on the flight that green and gold were the colours of Australia, but she still didn't match his mental image of an Australian any more than the streets she led him down, lined with trees bright with autumn leaves, fitted his notions of the land they called the sun-burnt country.

He took from her the small bag she was carrying and

matched her pace, walking silently, unwilling to prompt her again, thinking his own thoughts.

Paige said, 'She's pregnant.'

He stopped dead, forcing her to turn back to him as he stumbled into a mess of incoherent, half-formed questions.

'She's what? *Madonna mia!* How—? When—?'

Paige stared at him, unable to believe the man's shock and disbelief.

'How the hell do you think she got pregnant?' she stormed. 'And as for when, I presume it was shortly after you were married. One thing I did get out of her was the wedding date. How any man could be so insensitive as to speak of taking a mistress before he'd been married less than three months is beyond me.'

Now he looked plain bewildered.

'Who spoke of taking a mistress?' he asked, rubbing at his temples as if to massage his brain into working order.

'You did—or you intimated as much!' Paige retorted, then she looked at him again and wondered, having second thoughts. 'Or Lucia understood that's what you said,' she amended.

Her explanation didn't seem to help his confusion.

'What, in the name of all that's holy, have my mistresses to do with Lucia?'

It was Paige's turn for bewilderment—only that was too weak a word. 'Flabbergasted' fitted better. She stared at him, carefully controlling a lower jaw which seemed inclined to drop to an open-mouthed gape of disbelief. She wanted to shake him—pummel him—felt her fingers tingle with an itch to belt some sense into him, but it was none of her business how he ran his life.

'I've got patients to see,' she muttered, turning away

from him and striding down the road. He caught up in two paces, so she let him have a short blast of the anger churning inside her. 'And if you don't understand how a young sensitive woman like Lucia would view your behaviour—would suffer enormous anguish over it—then I'm certainly not wasting my breath telling you.'

They walked in silence for a few minutes, then he said, 'OK, so she's pregnant. Let's forget the other nonsense and proceed from there. I know I reacted badly to that news. Anyone would.'

Another mind-boggling concept—and one she had to refute.

'Not in Australia!' Again she stopped and faced him, wondering how a man who looked so good could be so shallow and fickle and downright stupid. 'Over here, prospective fathers are usually delighted to receive the news that their wives are pregnant. Most even put on a show of concern for them.'

His frown drew his eyebrows together in a slightly satanic manner.

'Prospective fathers? What does the reaction of prospective fathers have to do with me?'

Paige shook her head. First a fairytale prince, now fantasy land! Did this man know nothing about the process of reproduction? Or was he assuming the child wasn't his?

'Lucia is eighteen weeks pregnant,' she said carefully, wondering if, in spite of his beautifully correct use of English, he didn't understand it as well as she'd assumed. 'Given the date of your wedding, I would say she became pregnant in the early days of your honeymoon.'

It was his turn to do the flabbergasted act.

'My wedding? My honeymoon? You think Lucia is my wife? That it was me she ran away from?'

Only he wasn't flabbergasted at all. He was laughing, his head thrown back and the deep rumbles of sound echoing up into the trees.

'Well, if you're not her husband, who are you?' Paige asked the question crossly, cutting across his mirth, shaken by this turn of events and by the effect of his glee on her already stretched nerves.

'I am Marco,' he said, with a funny little bow. 'Lucia's loving and long-suffering brother. And knowing that, Miss Morgan, shall we start again?'

He held out his hand in a formal gesture and, reluctantly, she took it.

'It's Paige, not Miss Morgan,' she said, wondering where her voice had gone, leaving the words to falter out in a breathless undertone.

'Now we are friends,' he announced with complete assurance. He tucked her hand into the crook of his arm. 'Already I've delayed you so first we visit your patients, then we talk about Lucia, her marriage, her husband, her pregnancy and her flight. For the moment, it is enough to have seen her and know she is safe.'

Paige tried to think of some objection, considered removing her hand from the warm place where it lay— asserting her independence—but her mind had fled back to the fantasy land and it was only with a strenuous effort of will that she managed to dredge up one weak objection to his plan.

'You can walk with me but you can't visit my patients.'

He cocked his head to one side as he looked down at her.

'They would not like a visit from a prince?'

His lips teased into a smile, and she shook her head, although she knew the three women she was about to see would all revel in a visit from a prince, no matter how ancient or meaningless his title was. All three were housebound and anything out of the usual could provide them with something to think and talk about for weeks to come.

'These are medical visits,' she said primly, not wanting to say no outright, but aware of the ethical considerations of taking strangers into her patients' homes.

'So a doctor could accompany you?' he asked. 'Even a visiting doctor?'

Her hand was feeling increasingly comfortable, and the close proximity of his body was creating havoc with her senses, so she didn't place any importance on his questions, assuming he was making conversation. She struggled to keep her end of it going so he wouldn't guess at her thoughts and feelings.

'Of course, if the patients agreed to see him.'

'Well, that is arranged,' he said, satisfaction purring in the deep tones of his voice. 'You will say I wish to see Australian medicine while in your country and ask if they will allow me in.'

She pulled her hand away and tucked it out of temptation's reach in the pocket of her jacket.

'I can't pretend you're a doctor just to get you inside a few Australian homes, however interested you may be. And why should you be interested anyway? The health service clients are poor people, not only poor financially but some are lacking the skills necessary to survive without help. This is not typical Australia you'd be seeing, and I don't know that it's right to put them…on display, I suppose, for you or anyone else.'

He didn't reply immediately, but frowned off into the distance as if trying to work out his answer. Or perhaps thinking in Italian and translating into English. She looked at the strong profile, the dark hair brushed back but with one lock escaping control to fall across his temple.

She was glad he wasn't married to Lucia!

Stupid thought!

'We have poor people in Italy as well,' he said, cutting into her self-castigation. 'And those who are inadequately equipped in living skills as well. I would not judge your country on what I see, but, with that said, shouldn't a country be judged on how it treats these very people? How it provides support so they can live fulfilling and worthwhile lives?'

She had to smile, having used the same argument so often herself.

'I agree,' she conceded, 'but it still doesn't make you a doctor.'

She walked on, because smiling at him—and having him smile back—had turned out to be a very bad idea.

'But I *am* a doctor,' he announced, catching up with her in three long strides and falling into step again.

Marco a doctor?

She glanced at him, at the erect carriage, the aristocratic head, and said, 'Rubbish! You're a prince. Mr Benelli said so, and even a girl from the back blocks of New South Wales can recognise royalty when she sees it!'

She spoke lightly, jokingly, although she half meant every word.

'The "prince" is a an old title handed down through my family—inescapable if one is the eldest son—but it isn't a job description, Paige Morgan, any more than "Miss" describes the work you do.'

'You *are* a doctor?'

Disbelief ran riot through the question, but again he bowed just slightly in reply.

'I am,' he said. 'Now, should we continue this delightful chat here on the street or walk on to visit your patients?'

She walked on, remembering Lucia's words... 'Marco always gets his way.'

CHAPTER THREE

'MY FIRST patient lives in here,' Paige said, stopping in front of a small bungalow tucked well back from the road and almost hidden behind huge cotoneaster bushes which had been allowed to run wild.

'Sleeping Beauty, presumably,' Marco remarked, and Paige glanced swiftly at him, recalling how often she'd had that thought herself.

'Almost,' she said. 'Mrs Bevan was fine up until five years ago when her husband fell ill. She then began to feel all the classic symptoms of panic attacks—accelerated heart rate, flushing, faintness, perspiring heavily—usually when the doctor called. By the time Mr Bevan died a year later, she was unable to leave the house without being overcome by these sensations—often fainting before she reached the gate.'

Paige pushed through the same gate as she spoke and looked around as she walked up the path. Time to get the Scouts here again to do some subtle trimming of the trees.

'Was she diagnosed as agoraphobic?' Marco asked. 'If so, she may not wish to see me. I will understand.'

Paige was still coming to terms with his apparent interest. This was the same man who'd arrogantly demanded access to his sister earlier—who'd wanted nothing more than to be out of this town and on his way back to his home country. Now he was walking the back streets of the town with Paige—*and* offering to wait outside.

'She hasn't seen a psychiatrist if you feel that's required for official diagnosis. And I don't think she'll object to your visit. She's more secure in her own home these days and even welcomes company—it's going beyond the garden gate which induces the anxiety.'

'And her treatment?' Marco pursued as Paige lifted her hand to ring the bell.

She shrugged one shoulder, uncomfortable with admitting that in this respect she'd failed.

'She's not receiving any—' The explanation was cut short by the door opening as far as the safety chain would allow.

'Hi, Mrs Bevan. It's Paige and I've someone with me, a visiting doctor from Italy. Would you like him to come in or shall I ask him to wait outside?'

'Not the prince?' Mrs Bevan responded in a breathless voice. 'Oh, my, oh, my!'

Paige could hear her fingers scrabbling against the wood, fiddling with the chain as she hurried to unlatch it—apparently anxious to provide a royal welcome.

'Yes, yes, bring him in. Mabel called on her way back from the centre and told me he was visiting you.' Mrs Bevan must have freed the chain at last for she flung open the door and all but bowed Marco into the hall. 'Said he came in such a lovely car and with a courtier and all, she said.'

Marco seemed to accept this evidence of grandeur with equanimity, standing back and indicating that Paige should go ahead, but she was rooted to the top step, praying Mrs Bevan wouldn't repeat any of the other things Mabel had told her—particularly about Paige being in need of a man.

A light touch on her shoulder propelled her forward—out of touching range—gabbling explanations and excuses no one in their right mind would understand. Not that Mrs Bevan had noticed. Oh, no, she was far too busy gazing in awe at her visitor, standing, her hands clasped in front of her apron, and staring at him as if he'd arrived clad in ermine robes—or whatever princes traditionally clad themselves in—complete with crown and sceptre.

Paige took control of herself and Mrs Bevan. She guided her patient to a chair, indicating to the visitor to take another, then looked around, wondering what she'd done with her bag. Perhaps not quite in control!

Marco guessed what she was seeking and held up the bag he'd carried, amused by her confusion and surprised by the older woman's reaction to his title. Not that he hadn't experienced it before. Even at home, where old titles were common, the older people—those who knew—still treated him as something special. But here in egalitarian Australia?

He introduced himself to their hostess and watched as Paige took out a small sphygmomanometer from the bag and wrapped a blood-pressure cuff around Mrs Bevan's arm.

'You have a problem with your blood pressure?' he asked the patient.

'It's old age,' she responded. 'Everything breaking down, and what does work usually hurts. I guess it will happen even to princes when they get old.'

'That's telling you,' Paige whispered to him, jotting down her findings on a card and tucking the equipment back into the bag. She smiled at her patient. 'Your blood pressure is fine today, Mrs B. You've obviously been taking the tablets. Now, what about exercise? Are you walking in the garden each day?'

Mrs Bevan beamed, first at Paige, then at Marco and said, as proudly as a child revealing a good mark at school, 'Ten times in the morning and another ten in the afternoon.'

'That's grand,' Paige responded, while Marco considered the bungalow's size and wondered if twenty might not have been a better target. 'Perhaps you could build it up to twelve this week. Or do a few quick turns after dinner as well.'

He nodded his head in acknowledgment that their thoughts were in tandem, realising that the nurse was treading very carefully with this particular patient.

While he chatted to Mrs Bevan, Paige checked some small bottles which were lined up on a bench at the end of the room, then turned back to announce they should be on their way.

'You've enough tablets to last until next week, but if you think of anything you need, give me a call,' she said as she tucked some slips of paper into her pocket. 'I'll see you tomorrow.'

Then, to Marco's astonishment, she bent and kissed the wrinkled cheek, before heading towards the door. He followed, so many questions flung up by this routine visit that he hoped the next patient lived a long way down the road.

'Is she on some form of anti-anxiety medication?' he asked as they made their way to the gate. 'Under a psychiatrist? Do you encourage her to go out? Have you used behaviour therapies at all to get her over the initial shock of being out of her own environment? What treatment is considered appropriate over here?'

She must have been surprised by his interest for she stopped abruptly and he ran into her—felt the softness of her body against his chest.

He put a hand on her shoulder to steady them both, told himself it was the softness of her jacket he'd felt, and why should he notice anyway? All women had soft bodies. She dodged away from his hand and half turned to face him.

'The answer to all but the last of your questions is no. Yes, all of those treatments are used here, but you have to remember that most people suffering from anxiety disorders are young, with the mean onset in the early twenties. The seriousness of the disorder necessitates drugs for many people and psychiatrists use the often harsh treatment judged necessary to alter behaviour because of a patient's youth and the fact that he or she should have a long and productive life ahead of them. Even then many refuse treatment, being unable to admit to illness by taking drugs or visiting a specialist.'

He considered this and shook his head.

'So Mrs Bevan's age means you don't bother treating her?' he demanded, angry for the gentle old woman who'd reminded him of his grandmother.

Paige waved a hand, indicating they should walk and talk, and he wondered if she, like he, thought better when her body was in motion. Following a pace behind her through the gate, his mind clipped the two words together in a different frame and decided her body in motion was a most attractive sight. In fact, the impression of slimness was misleading as she undoubtedly had curves in all the right places. Plump curve of hips tapering into a tiny waist he could perhaps span with his hands—not that he could see her waist under the bulky jacket, but he'd noticed earlier—

'Pardon?'

She turned her head and smiled at him—that warm and genuine smile he'd observed and admired earlier.

'I've just produced a perfect explanation for not treating Mrs Bevan—or at least treating her in a way that's beyond the parameters of so-called normal therapy—and you haven't heard a word of it. Are you worrying about Lucia?'

Her brows, a darker gold than her hair, twitched together, and when he answered with a slight negative movement of his head she provided him with another excuse for his inattention.

'You must be tired,' she said. 'And here I am dragging you all over town, visiting the elderly.'

He shook his head again, denying tiredness but glad he didn't have to explain the real cause of his distraction.

She walked on and he caught up with her.

'I was saying we've tackled Mrs Bevan differently, encouraging her to have people in, to accept visitors. At first it was difficult as her husband's illness had isolated her, but as you saw today even a stranger didn't upset her unduly. And I've got her exercising in the yard. She's keen on birds, and always knows where the nests are in her garden. I live in hope that one day a bird will tempt her beyond the gate, and when she's done it once, it might become easier.'

'And have you constructed the nest of the bird beyond her boundary yet and trained the bird to fly above her towards the gate?'

He saw her shoulders move and heard the soft chuckle which escaped her.

'Don't think I haven't considered it,' she told him. 'But, like so many people with psychological problems, I have to move very slowly with her. Another friend, knowing of her interest in birds, gave her a canary in a cage, thinking it would be company for her. Mrs Bevan was horrified and made me find a good home for it. She couldn't bear the thought of a living creature being imprisoned like that, yet it's how she lives herself.'

'Perhaps that's why she was upset by it. Perhaps she has more insight into her self-imposed bars than you credit her with.'

He spoke gently, for he was moved by the compassion of this woman towards this particular patient. True, most nurses had compassion by the bucket-load, but Paige Morgan seemed to go an extra step. Which reminded him…

'And how does she exist? Who shops for her? She has sons, daughters, family?'

There was no answer from his guide, and he remembered the pieces of paper she'd tucked into her pocket.

'You?'

She glared at him.

'Well, someone has to and it's no bother for me to get her things when I'm shopping for myself,' she said defiantly.

'So someone else has told you you're stepping beyond professional duty,' he teased, enjoying the colour temper brought to her cheeks.

'You can't draw lines and boundaries in community care,' she retorted, pausing with her hand on another gate—this one leading into the yard of what looked like a block of apartments. 'What should I do? Starve her out of her house? Refuse to let people shop for her until she's desperate and has to overcome her fears in order to eat? Perhaps that's some people's way, but it isn't mine. The poor darling had no children, her husband was everything to her, then he died and left her so ill-prepared for life it's not surprising she began to panic.'

'And has been panicking ever since,' he said softly. 'I am not judging or condemning you. In fact, it is admiration I feel—for your understanding, and your willingness to take that extra step so many professionals, myself included, sometimes fail to realise needs taking! We tend to hope some safety net spread by someone else will catch these people, but all too often there is no net.'

Paige forgot about old Miss Wilde who would be peering through the lace curtains of the lower floor apartment, waiting anxiously for her to arrive.

'You sound as if you've experienced the ''no net'' phenomenon.' She probed cautiously for there'd been emotion in his voice.

'Had experience of it—seen the effects of it—fought with government officials about the implications of not having one—or not having it spread far enough,' he admitted, his voice abrasive with remembered anger.

'Someone close to you?' she asked. She couldn't have hidden her surprise very well for his reply was first a bark of laughter, then a gruff, 'You're surprised I should know such people? Being born with a title doesn't necessarily mean being born with wealth and, although my family was—is—well off thanks to my father's and grandfather's business acumen, not all our friends and associates are as fortunate. Yes, I've known people who have slipped through the welfare system and not been fortunate enough to have a Paige Morgan there to hold out a hand in friendship and support.'

He spoke stiffly, as if unused to speaking of such personal matters, and Paige guessed the person who had suffered had been close to him. A relative perhaps? Too proud to ask for help?

Embarrassed by his words, she walked towards the front door of the apartment building, thinking about the contradictions she'd seen in this man who strode beside her.

You only had to look at his face to know he'd be the

same as the person of whom he spoke, should bad times ever descend upon his shoulders.

'Well, Miss Wilde isn't afraid to speak out when she needs something, but she's hearing impaired and, although she's tried a variety of hearing-aids, she's too sensitive to the noise they make to persevere with wearing them.'

'So she stays at home? Does this make sense to you as well as her? Is it only I who cannot understand it?'

Paige grinned at his confusion.

'She isn't a permanent stay-at-home,' she explained. 'Actually, she has a better social life than I do, but she's laid up with gout at the moment so I said I'd drop in a new bottle of tablets for her. Be careful what you say to her. She'll get on to Henry the Eighth if you give her the slightest encouragement and regale you with tales of other royal gout sufferers.'

'Henry the Eighth? The English king of many wives?'

Paige watched the way his brow wrinkled in puzzlement and realised all his facial expressions were of interest to her. Probably because he was so impossibly good-looking, she had to keep watching in case one made him look ordinary.

She nodded. 'He was also known for his fits of temper when enduring the pain caused by his overindulgence in good food and even better wine,' she explained, but the frown deepened on his forehead and she guessed he was thinking of something far removed from gout.

'Alex said he'd take a mistress? *That's* why Lucia ran away? I can't believe it!'

Sorry she'd pressed the button that would light a globe inside Miss Wilde's apartment and let her know they were there, Paige faced him. She could follow Marco's mental leap from King Henry to Lucia's indiscreet husband, but to discuss it here and now?

'Well, he must have, or she wouldn't have been so upset.'

Blue eyes stared fixedly into hers.

'No man would do such a thing!' he declared, as if his conviction should wipe the whole scenario from both their minds.

'Say it, or take a mistress?' Paige asked, smiling at his delayed reaction to something she'd explained some hours ago.

'Both!' he said firmly, then actually had the grace to look embarrassed when she laughed.

'Well, not consider taking a mistress while still, more or less, on his honeymoon,' he amended, but before Paige could pursue the subject Miss Wilde arrived at the door, seated in a wheelchair, her left leg, with its grossly swollen foot and ankle, propped on a box-like contraption in front of her.

'Is this the prince?' she asked Paige in a voice which could have been heard four blocks away.

'What did you do, alert the town crier?' Marco demanded in an undertone.

'It was your fault for coming into the clinic,' she told him, before introducing him to Miss Wilde, being careful to speak slowly and face the woman as she formed the words.

'Come in, come in.'

As Miss Wilde began to turn in the direction of her front door, it was Marco who took control, swinging her carefully around and pushing her towards the open door on the far side of the foyer.

'In there?' He threw the words over his shoulder to

Paige, who had to stop admiring his straight back and broad shoulders and work out what he was talking about.

'Oh, yes, just through that door,' she floundered.

They were the last words she said for forty minutes. It turned out that Miss Wilde, ex-history teacher at the local high school, had a fascination with Italian history, so royal gout was passed over in favour of Italian royal lineage. She had Marco write down his full name and lineage then dissected it, pointing out the different dynastic families who had contributed to his gene pool and regaling them both with risqué tales of the more notorious members.

'We have to go,' Paige said at last, interrupting the flow when she realised it was getting late and she had another visit before she could return home.

Miss Wilde protested, but Marco must have sensed Paige's anxiety and he politely but firmly said his farewells then guided her towards the door.

'You are concerned about time? Is it Lucia who worries you? Do you not like leaving her alone? Would you wish me to return to the house to be with her?'

'I'm more concerned about her meal,' she explained. 'I try to keep them as regular as possible.' The words were no sooner out than she realised she hadn't explained the added complication of Lucia's pregnancy. And couldn't now, with one more visit to make. 'But, no, we still have time to visit Mrs Grantley. She's not much of a talker and has Mr Grantley for company. Actually, it's him I visit. I shower him and dress him ready for bed.'

'Perhaps I could do the task for you,' Marco offered, and Paige looked at him in surprise. Whether he'd worn a three-piece suit, made, she suspected, out of the finest quality wool, for the long flight to Australia, she didn't know, but she could hardly see him showering the easily agitated Mr Grantley in it.

'I'll manage,' she said dryly. 'Mr Grantley and I have a system. Here's the house. I'll introduce you to Mrs Grantley and you can chat to her while I fix her husband.'

Marco was smiling as they left the house half an hour later.

'And what's the system?' he enquired with exaggerated politeness. 'You get under the shower with him?'

Damn! She'd huddled quickly back into her jacket when the job was done, hoping he wouldn't notice how wet her clothes were.

She tilted her chin and assumed what she hoped was an expression of great dignity. 'Some days I don't get wet at all.'

Dignity got her nowhere for he continued to smile as he loped along beside her.

'Not that wet clothes don't do something for a woman,' he remarked, making her hug the jacket even closer. 'Although you shouldn't be wandering out in the cold night air in such dampness. Is there no kind of protection you could wear? A raincoat, for instance?'

Paige sighed, knowing that what he said made sense and that the regular community nurses always wore protection.

'I don't want to make it look as if I'm someone come in to bathe him,' she muttered, although she knew the words probably wouldn't make any sense to him. 'He seems to react better with me—usually—because he sees me as a friend, and although his mind is affected by dementia he has good days and good moments. On a good day, he'd be appalled to think I had to wear a raincoat to help him in the shower.'

She received no answer. Perhaps Marco had been

thinking of something else and hadn't heard her limp explanation.

Well, she wasn't going to repeat it, she decided, as she quickened her pace to keep up with his long strides.

'You like to make sure Lucia has regular meals?' He stopped walking and turned to face her. 'You must excuse me for catching up with your information so slowly. I can only suppose it is fatigue from the flight—a delayed reaction that is slowing my thought processes. Lucia has been ill during this pregnancy? Yes, she looked ill. She has been nauseous, vomiting, unable to retain food? Is she seeing a specialist? How is he treating her? Not with drugs, I assume?'

He sounded so anxious—so annoyed with himself for not asking more questions earlier—that Paige laid a hand on his arm and said, 'She's certainly under specialist care and she's so much better now you needn't be overly concerned.' She paused, not wanting to shock him further yet knowing she couldn't protect him from the truth.

'She's suffering from gestational diabetes mellitus.' There, it was out. She watched his face as he absorbed this information and ran it through his mind, probably dredging up half-forgotten facts from his student days—unless he had specialised in either obstetrics or illnesses such as diabetes.

'But it's too early to know that,' he protested. 'You said what? Eighteen weeks?'

Paige nodded then walked on.

'Yes, but apparently it can come on earlier than the usual twenty-four- to twenty-eight-week onset.' She hesitated, wanting to make the explanation as concise as possible but not wanting to alarm him too much.

'She's only been with me a month,' she began. 'I'm not certain when she arrived in Australia but I do know she spent some time in Melbourne and later in Sydney with a lass she met on the plane. Then, when a group of young people decided to take the outback coach, she joined them. Unfortunately, within ten days of travelling with them, she was feeling ill enough for these friends to be concerned about her health and to tell the coach captain, who brought her to the health service.'

'Where you took her in!'

He shook his head as if this was the least understand-able aspect of the saga.

'She was desperately ill. Not eating properly, having fainting spells. In fact, if the group hadn't carried a con-stant supply of sweets and offered them to her whenever she was strong enough to suck something, she might have been worse off. Or perhaps the condition didn't surface until just before she arrived here. A form of morning sickness, which I gather went on all day and was aggra-vated by and mistaken for motion sickness, would have depleted her body of nutrients even without the drain of foetal needs.'

'And now?' he demanded. 'Is she able to balance her blood glucose by diet alone? Is she exercising?' He struck his forehead with the heel of his hand. 'Stupid question! When did Lucia ever exert a milligram more energy than she need?'

'Well, she is exercising, as it happens,' Paige told him, hurrying the pace now they were back in sight of her home. 'I explained how important it was.'

'And she took notice of you?' Marco demanded, dis-belief ringing in the deep register of his voice.

'Well, actually, no, but when I talked about losing her figure after the baby is born, she did agree to follow some simple routines. I hired a walking machine as I've been reluctant to let her walk the streets on her own. I'm not sure how much experience you've had of pregnant diabetic patients but, unfortunately, by keeping the blood sugar under control you get an added risk of hypoglycaemia—dizzy spells, loss of consciousness—if not treated quickly.'

'You hired a walking machine?'

This time the disbelief was tinged with mirth and he'd totally ignored all her medical explanations.

'Well, it was all I could think of for her,' Paige muttered defensively. 'And I might add that although you seem to be finding this amusing none of it's been very funny from my side of the fence.'

He immediately looked chastened, and rested a hand on her shoulder as if in apology.

'I can understand your position, and I do not laugh at you,' he said, that fascinating voice now as deep and soft and smooth as the most expensive chocolate. 'I and my family will be eternally grateful to you for taking care of Lucia. It is simply that you keep surprising me with your—your resourcefulness! Are all Australians as practical and filled with common sense?'

Night had fallen swiftly but they had halted where the streetlight threw a buttery wedge of light around them, casting the darkness beyond its reach into darker shadows. But not as dark as those which hid his eyes.

Paige stared at him, wondering why the question should make her feel so downhearted. Was it because common sense didn't usually feature as a prerequisite for the heroines in fairytales? Because she'd rather he thought her ravishingly beautiful than sensible?

Not that she *was* ravishingly beautiful, of course.

'Well?' he prompted, looking down at her, seeing more of her than she could of him because the light fell on her face. 'Can you not answer or are you too modest to explain you are one among few?'

She shrugged the question away and said lightly, 'I don't think kindness is defined by nationality. Faced with an ill young woman, anyone would have done the same thing.' She thought of the weirdos who infected every society and amended the sentence. 'Almost anyone!'

That made him laugh again, attracting the attention of Lucia who must have been waiting for their return. A window above them opened and her head appeared in the aperture.

'Marco. Paige. Hello to you. I was worrying. I slept then woke and feel very well indeed.' She was bubbling with excitement, not even waiting for an answer to her greeting before continuing. 'I have had a so wonderful idea. Because you have been so kind to me, Paige, Marco will take us both to dinner. You said you knew an Italian restaurant you would take me to when I was well—and now I am well, so we shall go. See…'

She leaned even further out, making Paige yell a warning to be careful lest she fall, but her words went unheeded as Lucia flung her arms wide.

'I am already dressed!'

'It's no good arguing with her,' Marco told Paige with enough gloom to convince her a dinner at the local Italian restaurant was the last thing he wanted. He ushered her towards the side door they'd used earlier. 'Much better just to go along. Has she a diet sheet? Does she know what she can and can't eat?'

Paige chuckled.

'You may know her well enough not to argue, but if you think either her specialist or myself could convince her of the importance of taking control of her own health requirements, then you're wrong. Your sister Lucia is far too used to being cared for to be even vaguely interested in dietary needs, nor have I persuaded her—so far—to do her own injections—even her own blood glucose tests.'

'But that's a simple matter—a prick of the finger.' Marco pointed out the obvious. 'I've known six-year-olds do it.'

'Not Lucia!' Paige corrected him, unlocking the door and letting them both into the downstairs hallway. 'But that's something you can rectify, I'm sure. After all, while you might think Lucia always gets her own way, she's equally convinced of your powers of persuasion. ''Marco *always* gets his way,'' she told me.'

She heard the words echo in the open space and regretted them, wishing she'd resisted the urge to tease him. He was too close—too masculine—too threatening in some undefined way. Paige shivered and felt his hands settle on her shoulders. She tried to pull away but her willpower had deserted her.

'Not always,' he said in a husky voice that felt like velvet in her ears.

'No?' The word squeaked out, betraying her agitation, although she was sure he could also hear her erratic heartbeat and feel the nerves jumping in her skin.

'No!' he whispered. 'Because right now Marco has an almost uncontrollable urge to kiss your lips—to see if they taste as sweet as they look. Of course, he would pretend it was a thank-you for caring for his sister—a casual salute. But he was brought up to treat a woman with respect so he won't do it, but it's proof—no? Proof that Marco doesn't always get his way.'

And on that most unexpected note he let her go, and stepped back out through the door.

'I shall return in half an hour. It is not too late for my sister to eat?'

Paige shook her head, completely bemused by the events of the entire day—shocked into silence by those of the last few minutes.

'Half an hour is fine,' she managed to mumble, but when he'd disappeared from sight she realised how little time she had to shower and change and yelled after him, 'And thanks for asking if it suited me as well!' Then she stomped crossly up the stairs, smiling at Lucia's excitement but inside annoyed with the woman for arranging that they go out, and with herself for letting a man she'd never see again get under her skin, and most of all with him, for...

Well, just with him!

CHAPTER FOUR

THERE was nothing in Paige's wardrobe she could remotely consider to be 'going out with a prince' gear so she settled on a tartan miniskirt she'd paid too much for at the fashion parades during the recent Wool Week, teaming it with a fine knit sweater in her favourite forest green.

The dark colour made her skin seem paler, but reflected more green into her eyes so they didn't look quite so much like stagnant creek water. Eschewing make-up, apart from mascara and lipstick, she took extra time to brush her hair. It mightn't curl and froth attractively around her shoulders, as Lucia's did, but with a bit of extra effort in the brush strokes at least it shone.

'You are ready, Paige?' Lucia called. 'Marco will be here any minute. He is never late.'

'Well, good for him,' Paige muttered to herself, wondering how she was going to face this paragon of punctuality again after that odd conversation in the downstairs hall.

Put it down to his tiredness, common sense told her, but no amount of common sense could quite extinguish the tiny flicker of warmth his words had fanned to life inside her.

'It's the reaction of any woman who's told she's seen as desirable,' she reminded herself. 'Don't make a big thing of it.'

But as she left the bathroom and walked with Lucia down the stairs, she could feel the heat from the flicker creeping upwards through her body—heading for her cheeks no doubt, where it would make it clear to even the most insensitive of men that she was uneasy—to put it mildly—in his presence.

Not that Marco seemed to notice. His arrival coincided with their descent and Lucia ran ahead to let him in. Politeness decreed that she offer him a drink, but he refused, saying he had the driver waiting in the car.

'Benelli has relations in the area and has arranged for both he and the driver to visit them this evening,' he added.

'Then we could take my car and I'll drop you back at your hotel later,' Paige suggested. 'That would save interrupting their evening.'

Marco seemed to find this suggestion unusual but when Paige pressed further, explaining that Lucia tired easily and would not be wanting a late night, he gave in and went out to speak to his 'courtiers' while Paige found her car keys.

'He's not used to being driven by a woman,' Lucia said gleefully as they set off on the short distance to the centre of the town. 'In fact, he refused to let me drive his car for practice when I was having lessons because he said women weren't meant to be drivers—they have too many things on their minds all the time to be able to concentrate.'

Paige glanced at her front-seat passenger, wondering how he was taking this apparently verbatim recital of his words. She saw a smile twitch at his lips and remembered the sound of his laughter. So, he liked a joke, even if it was against him, she decided, and smiled herself.

She pulled up in front of the restaurant and was flattered to find princely good manners extended to him first opening the rear door for his sister, then walking around to hold hers as she alighted.

'Thank you,' she said, wondering how long it had been since someone performed this probably meaningless courtesy for her. She had usually driven when she and James had gone out, as he'd considered a few drinks part of his relaxation routine, but he'd have wondered why she'd been taking so long getting out of the car if she'd waited for him to open the door.

In fact, he'd probably have assumed she'd lost something—and seen it as yet another example of her failure to conform to his expectations of her.

'May we sit in the courtyard out the back?' Lucia asked, peering in through the door and spying the open area beyond the main restaurant.

'Miss Morgan may prefer warmth to a draughty courtyard,' Marco replied, while Paige wondered why he'd reverted to formality.

Well, it explained him opening the car door—formality, nothing more. And why? No doubt tiredness and relief to be reunited with his sister had prompted that strange exchange, and in hindsight he'd retreated behind a wall of good manners.

'The courtyard is only open in summer,' she told Lucia, playing peacemaker before an argument began. 'Hello, Mrs Ryan. These are friends of mine—Marco and Lucia. Do you have a table for three?'

'Mrs Ryan? Now there's a good Italian name,' Marco whispered as the short, square-built woman with elaborately coiffed white hair led them to a small table at the rear of the room, and dropped three menus into the centre of it.

'She was Theresa Agnelli before she married Tom Ryan,' Paige explained. 'Although Tom does the cooking, she's the guiding force and, with her mother, taught him most of what he knows. In fact, her mother helped out in the restaurant until last year.'

'Last year? Her mother? Your Mrs Ryan looks well into her sixties.'

Paige grinned at him. He might have reverted to formality but he seemed genuinely interested in the little details of lives which touched his—even remotely.

'Mrs Ryan's sixty-eight, and still as spry and active as most forty-year-olds. She's organised a number of local people into growing vegetables for her and every morning drives around to visit them and select what she wants for the day's meals.'

Marco's brow creased.

'Small farms? Benelli showed me grazing land for sheep and cattle, but when I asked he said there are no smallholdings in this area.'

'It's not farmers Mrs Ryan visits, but ordinary householders who have vegetable plots in their backyards.' OK, so it wasn't riveting conversation, but at least talking distracted her thoughts from his blue eyes. 'In fact, we have two houses built to cater for the needs of young people with disabilities, and their gardens produce all the herbs and many of the rarer vegetables Mrs Ryan wants. Things like okra, which isn't widely grown here.'

'This is not the talk I wish to hear,' Lucia said, breaking into a conversation which didn't centre on her needs before Marco could answer. 'I want to talk of food and what we shall all eat now I'm finally out in the real world again. I shall have salad and then cake,' she announced, dropping her menu on the table and glancing at Paige, as if expecting her to argue, then at Marco, seeking an ally when it happened.

Paige pushed the menu back towards her.

'You will have a proper meal first—then perhaps Mr Ryan's diet zabaglione,' she said firmly. 'I know he makes it with an aspartame sweetener.'

'Seems my headstrong young sister has finally met her match,' Marco said, and received a glare from Lucia in reply.

'Not at all,' Paige replied. 'Lucia understands that to stay well she must watch what she eats, balance her calorie intake, restrict her fats and cut out simple sugars. That's the only way the insulin will be effective in controlling her blood glucose levels.'

Marco realised Paige was repeating this for Lucia's sake, not his, and wondered what battles had been fought to bring his sister to even this level of reluctant compliance. As Paige slipped a sheet of paper he guessed might be a diet substitution chart from her pocket and placed it unobtrusively beside her menu, he knew she'd taken on a bigger job than he'd imagined—especially given Lucia's partiality for sweets and chocolates.

'And what do you recommend for me?' he asked Paige, closing his menu and letting her decide his food intake as well.

'Let's ask Mrs Ryan what the speciality is tonight,' she suggested. 'Maybe we could all have that.'

'No, I'll have pasta,' Lucia argued. 'With broccoli, sun-dried tomatoes and pine nuts.' She poked out her tongue at Paige as if to say 'so there' then added with a long-suffering sigh, 'And the zabaglione!'

Used to his sister's behaviour when thwarted, Marco was more interested in Paige's reaction to what amounted to rudeness no matter how teasing the gesture had been. But the nurse—well, he assumed she was a trained nurse—took no notice but checked the menu once more, comparing it to the list she carried, then turning as Mrs

Ryan approached the table to consult with her about the specials for the evening.

A supremely unflappable young woman—or one who'd summed up Lucia very quickly and had learned that the best way to deal with his sister's behaviour was to ignore it. She intrigued him—this Paige Morgan. Even her name—Paige. Plain, yet soft—serene. He liked serenity—perhaps all the more because his family, himself included, were inclined to be excitable.

'It's a kind of stew,' she said, and he had to give himself a mental shake to remember what they were discussing. 'The special tonight. Like osso bucco but without the bones is how Mrs Ryan explained it.'

He nodded, catching up on the conversation before he made a fool of himself and letting Paige order for all of them. But after that she seemed to withdraw, allowing Lucia to take over, asking him questions about the family and their friends.

'I shouldn't answer you,' Marco replied, keeping his face stern but unable to stop smiling inside—so glad was he to see this irresponsible but much-loved sister. 'You've shown you didn't care about any of them, going off like that and not letting anyone know where you were.'

'I phoned Mama,' she answered sulkily. 'And asked a friend who was going to back to Italy to phone her as well.'

He must be tireder than he thought. He glanced at Paige and received a slight lift of her shoulders—a signal that said, 'I don't know about that.'

Nice shoulders but he had to follow through on Lucia's words, not be distracted by the shapely body parts of a woman he would never see again.

'You phoned Mama?' he repeated. 'When?'

'All the time. I told her not to tell a soul. I said I wouldn't phone again if she told you or anyone else and she knew I meant it. And I didn't tell her I was in Australia. The phone calls go straight through so I let her think I was travelling in Europe with some friends, but we didn't talk much about where I was and I couldn't tell her about the baby or she'd have got hysterical. She was already very angry with me.'

'Don't strangle her here in public,' Paige murmured. 'If you leave it until we get back to my place I'll say it was justifiable homicide. In fact, I may even help. I imagine it's my phone bill she's been running up with these clandestine calls.'

'*Por amor di Dio.*' He bit back a second, even worse oath and frowned at Paige, then turned his attention back to Lucia who at least had the grace to look embarrassed. He couldn't decide which crime was worse—his mother's deceit about this contact, although she had kept assuring him Lucia would be all right and he had wondered that she hadn't been more distressed, or Lucia calmly using someone else's phone, especially when that someone had already rescued her from who knew what kind of fate.

'If Mama had told you, you would have told Alex, or at least insisted I go home.'

'Which I shall,' he said grimly, then sat back as Mrs Ryan arrived with a plate of antipasto.

'Paige says I am too ill to travel,' Lucia snapped, ignoring the woman serving them and glaring her defiance across the table. 'I will stay here.'

'Dependent on a stranger's kindness for all your needs?'

Paige heard the disbelief in Marco's voice and turned her attention to the food, carefully considering the delights offered before selecting a piece of melon wrapped in prosciutto. The longer she could stay out of this sibling argument the better.

'Paige enjoys having me!'

With reservations, she thought, and heard Marco growl his rebuttal.

'Enjoys having to work out your menu every day, weigh your food, test your blood, probably give you your injections? Perhaps if you were self-sufficient and offered help to her she might just tolerate your company, but enjoy?'

She didn't have to glance towards Lucia to know that tears would be gathering in her eyes. Time to cut it short. She'd experienced her guest's emotional outbursts before and was too tense to cope with the dramatics of one tonight.

'Arguing won't achieve much. And Lucia is right when she says it would be unwise to travel right now. In a week or so perhaps, when we've more idea of the correct insulin levels she needs to keep in balance, but even then the journey would have to be strictly supervised to prevent either hyper- or hypoglycaemia.'

She looked at Marco, and wondered if she would be mad to voice her next thought—to encourage him to stay when he was disrupting her usually controllable body after half a day in town. She did it anyway!

'I know you spoke of having to get back to Italy, but could you delay a week? I can give you details of her regimen, and by then you'd know how it all works. I think she'll need qualified support on hand to undertake the long flight safely whenever she goes.'

'I will not go back with Marco, like a child dragged home by her big brother,' Lucia stormed. 'It is none of his business. It is not Marco who should take me back, but Alex! After all, it was his fault I had to go!'

'And a great lot of help he'd be,' Marco growled, his frustration so apparent Paige wondered they couldn't see it like a huge red cloud hovering above his head. 'He's as infantile as you are, Lucia. Does nothing but sit around and weep that you are gone. Day in and day out, phoning me to weep across the airwaves when no one else will listen to him.'

Paige pulled a face at Marco's description of this limp behaviour of the deserted groom but Lucia seemed delighted at the image, clapping her hands and uttering, 'Oh, does he really weep?' It was said in such melodramatic tones that Paige had to wonder if they might not deserve each other.

'All the time!' Marco assured her, although his voice suggested he found the behaviour more repugnant than delightful.

'Perhaps I *shall* go back to him!' Lucia announced. 'But he must come for me, and then something must be arranged. I think you are right about him helping me, though. He would not be so good with diets or tests or injections because he would not wish to hurt me.'

'More fool he,' Marco told her darkly. 'If you were my wife, I'd ring your neck for all the trouble you've caused in a fit of pique. And don't tell me about what he said or did, because I don't believe anything short of whipping you could have been enough justification to excuse your behaviour. And even that might not have been such a bad idea.'

The thought made Paige shiver, not entirely from discomfort. She waited for Lucia to erupt in her own defence, but the young woman remained silent, suspiciously so, toying with an olive, piercing it with her fork and rolling it around the plate, her gaze abstracted.

'I know!' she said at last. 'I have the most wonderful idea. Tonight you will phone Alex, Marco, and tell him where I am so he can begin his journey to rescue me, and Paige, who has months and months of holidays coming soon—beginning in one week, I think she said—will fly to Italy with us to make me eat the right things and do my finger-pricks and injections.' She clapped her hands at this example of her own cleverness and beamed at both of them. 'Is not that a grand idea?'

'No!'

'No!'

If anything, Paige decided, her no had marginally beaten Marco's, but unfortunately she couldn't think of anything to back it up. She was too stunned by Lucia's proposal and her apparent belief that both the erring Alex and the patient Paige would unquestioningly fall in with her plans.

'You cannot ask this of a woman who has already given so much of her time and patience to care for you.' Apparently Marco wasn't having trouble finding words. 'Which reminds me. Have you contributed to her housekeeping for your food? Have you even offered to pay board?'

'I took Lucia in as a guest,' Paige protested.

Lucia said furiously, drowning Paige's words, 'She asked me to stay.'

'That's getting off the subject,' Paige persisted. 'I need no repayment for a simple kindness. In fact, I've enjoyed Lucia's company.'

She ignored the dark eyebrows which flew upwards at this declaration—and the quizzical gleam in the eyes beneath them. Telling herself that good looks and smiling eyes weren't everything in a man, she went on, 'There are services which would provide a trained nurse to travel with Lucia if you can't change your plans to accompany her home.'

'May I ask one more kindness?' Marco asked, the smile she'd seen in his eyes playing about his lips. 'That you furnish me with the address or contact number of such a service so I may speak with them before I leave.'

He glanced at Lucia, sighed, then rubbed his fingers through his hair, disturbing the smoothness of it and causing that wayward lock to fall forward again. But when he spoke again it was to Paige, not his sister.

'I have to attend a conference in Switzerland at which I am speaking. That is the reason why I cannot further delay my return. I have no doubt that Alex, being as foolish as Lucia, is already making plans to come out here. I phoned him this afternoon. Can you put up with her until she is able to travel? And handle things once a decidedly damp groom arrives to offer his apologies?

'I don't envy you the job and wouldn't blame you if you moved her immediately into a hotel with a nurse-carer to look after her. Her husband's tears won't stop simply because he knows she is safe. If my phone call to him this afternoon was any indication, he will weep more than ever at the fond reunion.'

Lucia slapped at him, but she was smiling at the same time, as if the thought of a weeping husband pleased her.

'She can stay with me as long as she wishes,' Paige promised, and received a rapturous smile from Lucia and another sardonic lift of eyebrows from her brother.

'I wouldn't allow her too much leeway,' he warned, then deftly turned the conversation, as if afraid she might change her mind. He asked about the health service, the extent of its operations and the source of its funding.

'It began as a drop-in centre for the people in the area—somewhere they could meet. A few new mothers organised a playgroup for their little ones, meeting four mornings a week in the room we use as a waiting room now.'

'There was nowhere else for them—no regular facility?'

His eyes told her he was interested, not just making idle conversation, so she explained.

'They could have used one of the local church halls, I suppose—in fact, there's another playgroup in town which does use church premises, but for a small group the hall is so large, and when attendance is irregular sometimes the person rostered to tidy up is away and it doesn't get done.'

He smiled suddenly, as if his mind had made the leap across all she hadn't said.

'So the church asked them to leave?'

'Got it in one,' she said, acknowledging his perception with a dip of her head. 'At the house, if it was a mess it wasn't a big mess, and more often than not whoever arrived first the next morning cleaned it up.'

His interest must have geared up a notch, for he leaned forward.

'Or whoever was living in your flat cleaned it up. Was the house always divided? Is it owned by your government or a local authority?'

He's only asking for the sake of conversation, she told herself, but 'the house' had become such a large part of her disagreements with James that she didn't want to discuss it.

'*Vitellone all cacciatore.*' Mrs Ryan saved her from answering, arriving at the table and setting an earthenware casserole down in the middle. 'I'll get the pasta

now, but the child should eat some vitellone as well.'
She patted her own solidly rounded stomach. 'Good for
baby.'

An even greater diversion!

Lucia turned on Paige. 'How could you tell her? Talk
about me like that behind my back? It was our secret,
Paige. Only you and me were to know. You promised
me!'

Paige reached out to touch her hand, but Lucia
snatched it away.

'I've told no one,' Paige told her. 'Some women seem
to be able to sense these things. I wouldn't break my
word.'

The explanation was plainly disbelieved by Lucia who
made small grunting noises and proceeded to sulk.

'We were talking about the house,' Marco persisted.
'Take no notice of that tantrum—she's behaving like the
child Mrs Ryan called her. Tell me how the arrangement
works.'

But the mood had shifted, Lucia's small outburst reminding Paige how little she knew of these people—and
how transient their contact was likely to be. Far from
pleasing her, the thought made her feel profoundly depressed, but she tried to sound cheerful as she responded.

'I think Lucia has reason to be upset. We're out for a
dinner to celebrate the two of you being reunited and you
and I are talking shop.' She turned to Lucia, asking about
the home to which she'd return, getting on to someone
else's house instead.

It wasn't until much later, when the meal was finished
and Lucia, exhausted by the excitement of the day, had
been taken home, had had her blood tested and had received her final longer-acting insulin injection which
would see her through the night, that Paige realised the

subject hadn't been dropped at all, merely shelved by this virtual stranger who was not only disrupting her hormones but seemed intent on delving into too many other aspects of her life.

She'd suggested dropping Marco back at the hotel on their way home, but, no, he had to see Lucia's routine, he'd said, in case Paige tossed her out into the street and he was left to handle it.

Lucia had pouted again, but as they'd walked to the car she'd clung to Paige's arm, and intuition had told Paige there was more to Lucia's behaviour than petulance. The young woman had probably been thrust into too many new situations too quickly in the last few months and was suffering from an emotional overload on top of her medical condition.

'Don't be too harsh on her,' she said to Marco when Lucia had finally retired and they were walking back down the stairs. She wondered if she should offer him coffee before driving him home. They'd said no at the restaurant but that had been because Lucia had been wilting.

The woman in her wanted him to stay—only because she enjoyed his company and his arrival had made her realise she missed male company—but the nurse could see the tiredness in the lines cut more deeply into his cheeks and the shadowy darkness beneath his eyes.

'I couldn't be harsh to Lucia no matter how much she deserved it,' he answered after a pause that made her wonder what he'd been thinking. They had reached the bottom of the stairs and stood in the wide hall, the area softly lit by wall sconces. 'And there's no need for you to drive me back to the hotel. I can walk—it isn't far and I've been this way often enough to know the direction.'

So much for wanting coffee! an inner voice jeered as Paige's chest tightened slightly with disappointment.

'What time are you going back to Sydney? When is your flight?'

He took her hand in his and bent his head as if to study her fingers.

'You are anxious to be rid of at least one Alberici? I do not blame you. I must leave your town by mid-morning and will catch an evening flight home, going via Athens. I will visit Lucia again in the morning, but…'

The hesitation seemed out of character but Paige refused to prompt him. Let him come out with whatever it was himself.

She did, however, extract her hand, thinking what a strange habit this handholding was, wondering if it was typically Italian.

He stepped back, looked down at her and smiled.

'Already we have imposed on you far too much, but if I could have a little more time. Perhaps a cup of coffee? Would you like to return to the restaurant to have it?'

Of course! she decided. He needs to know more of Lucia's condition, of the regimen we've been following—that's why he wants to stay.

'I could make you coffee,' she offered. 'Real coffee, not instant, but I'm not sure if it's the type you'd prefer.'

His reply was a devastating smile. 'You ask that question of a fellow professional who has endured untold cups of the liquid hospitals call coffee? I have often considered doing a paper on it—how so many medical institutions in all parts of the globe have developed the same recipe for ruining what is such a simple drink to make.' The smile twinkled in his eyes in a way that made her stomach go into spasms and her heart begin to jitterbug.

'I'll make you coffee,' she muttered, almost running

from him, into the kitchen, busying herself, anything to prevent him guessing at her agitation.

'You want to know more about Lucia's health,' she said, when he followed her and seemed intent on helping, standing too close—getting in her way, affecting the air in some way that made it difficult for her to breathe. 'I can contact Jim Edgar, her obstetrician, and see if he can see you before he begins his rounds in the morning.'

Her companion nodded casually.

'That was to be my first question—I would appreciate you making arrangements—but it is not my main interest, for other doctors than I will be treating Lucia.'

He paused, and she waited, unable to guess what might be coming, knowing only that the sooner he was out of her house—and her life—the sooner she could return to normal. She grinned to herself, wondering if Cinderella had felt the same way as she'd fled from the ball—too far out of her league to be comfortable.

He moved away, circling the kitchen like a dog did its territory, then he selected one of the armchairs in front of the stove, shifting about until he'd comfortably disposed of his length in its depths. But all the time he watched her, and she felt his interest—not personal man-woman stuff, but interest nonetheless.

She put the two cups of coffee on the small table between the armchairs and sat down herself.

'My interest is in this house,' he told her.

'This house?' She couldn't have been more startled if he'd expressed an interest in Abyssinian ants—if such things existed. 'It's just a house—typical of many built about a hundred years ago when the town was first established. Merchants, doctors, lawyers—all the more financially successful people in town—went in for sturdy brick construction and, because they generally had large families, they built big.'

He was smiling at her in a way that made the blood sing in her veins, but she wasn't going to be diverted by musical blood and was about to explain her great-grandfather's design when he interrupted her.

'It isn't the actual building that draws my attention, but the services it offers to the community. You began to tell me of this playgroup. What is that?'

Easy question! She explained the system which enabled mothers of young and very young children to meet, providing interaction for their children, some guided play activities and an informal support group for the mothers.

'Older women pass on their experience, the women share solutions to common problems, tell what works for them in things that range from mastitis to infant colic to where to buy baby clothes made with natural fibres. The conversation ranges far and wide, and the children learn some socialising skills. It's not as formal as a kindergarten situation, and provides a sense of security for the children, allowing them to move beyond their normal boundaries because their mothers—or sometimes fathers—are present.'

'So, it began with a playgroup. Did the owner of the house simply say, "I have a house with too many rooms—you may use one of them for this purpose"?'

She felt a frown pluck at her eyebrows. It *was* the house that was interesting him. But why?

'Yes, more or less,' she told him, then she picked up her coffee and sipped at it, determined to ignore the invisible undercurrents zapping her body. They were so strong she wondered if it was possible he couldn't feel them—but then, he had the kind of body which would zap unwary females every minute of every day, so why should he be aware of her reaction?

'Then the owner said, "Please, use another room for a nurse to see people"?' The smile accompanying the words did strange things to her toes.

But why the questions?

Paige considered how best to answer. How to reply at all when tingling toes were demanding her attention.

'More or less,' she replied, then guessed he wasn't going to leave it there. 'The town had, and still has, regular community health services—nurses who visit bed-ridden patients, meals-on-wheels for the elderly or those who find preparing meals difficult for other reasons. We have an outpatients service at the hospital which provides free medical attention, but...'

'But?'

His deep voice seemed to her disordered sense to caress the word.

'But it lacked cohesion.' She blurted out the words. 'No one knew what anyone else was doing—the safety net we spoke about earlier was strung so loosely there were huge gaps. The playgroup mothers began referring each other to different people and places.

'For instance, they talked about toys which helped their children's development, then someone realised that not all the families attending had the money to provide what are often very expensive age-oriented toys. And what did families whose children had passed that age group do with the old toys? The idea of a toy library came from that. It needed housing so they took over another room for that.'

She stopped abruptly, actually remembering those times when it had seemed new ideas were floated every day and everyone involved had been fired with so much enthusiasm the place had tingled with its energy.

'Go on,' he prompted, pushing his empty coffee cup away and settling back in his chair as if he had all night to listen to her prattle on about something that couldn't possibly interest him.

'We had a child with cerebral palsy, others lagging behind in their fine motor development. One of the occupational therapists at the hospital offered to come one morning a week to work with these children and select the best toys for them to take home.'

He chuckled. 'Now I am beginning to understand—I can see it spreading out like honey spilled from a jar. What other services are offered here? Do all the professionals volunteer? And who pays for the house—its rent, upkeep?'

Easy stuff this. In fact, the conversation would have been enjoyable, for she was proud of what her ad hoc group had achieved, if her mind hadn't been constantly diverted by her physical responses to this man.

'We have an aromatherapist, a physio, two other people who do therapeutic massage, one qualified doctor who also practices acupuncture and four other doctors who volunteer one afternoon a week to see patients who find the waiting time at the hospital too difficult to handle or who don't wish to go there for some other reason. And, yes, they all work for nothing.'

'And you, Paige Morgan? What is your place in all of this?'

Another smile, even more devastating than the first. Paige steeled herself against it.

'I try to draw it all together,' she explained. 'I do normal nurse stuff like dressings or injections, inoculation of the infants, that kind of thing. I also talk to people, screen those who wish to see a doctor, direct others to whatever service might prove most helpful to them. I'm officially the co-ordinator but I'm more a go-between.'

'And pay? You obviously work full time here. Is it for wages? Do the patients contribute? Does your government provide?'

She was bemused by his interest but answered anyway. Talking kept her mind off the way his fingers were intertwined, the way his hands lay so still on his knees— kept it off thinking of the warmth she'd felt when he'd held her hand in his.

'At first it was voluntary but now the government funds the co-ordinator's and the receptionist's positions and many of the patients contribute. We don't ask for money, but there's a coin box on the front counter and people drop what they can afford into it.'

'And it works?' he demanded.

She was surprised by his tone but nodded.

He sighed, then shook his head.

'It is amazing that something which has grown with so little forethought and organisation should succeed when so often similar initiatives provided by the government, in Italy anyway, have failed.'

'You know that for a fact?' she asked, startled by his statement. 'You've been involved in such a failure?'

Surely not. Studying him again, she found it impossible to link the word 'failure' with him.

'Involved in the theoretical exercise that preceded setting it up, not in its implementation,' he admitted, and sighed again.

'So Marco doesn't always get his way,' Paige said softly, but her guest didn't reply, and when she looked at him she realised his head had dropped forward onto his chest. She wasn't going to get a reply. He was asleep.

CHAPTER FIVE

PAIGE knew she should wake Marco and drive him to his hotel so he could get a proper night's rest, but she hesitated, wanting to look at him, to think about his sudden— and very temporary—advent into her life. And her reaction to it.

It's a sign I'm over James. Perhaps ready to socialise more, mix and mingle, go out with men.

She shuddered, amended the word to the singular and looked at her guest again. Prince or no prince, most men would pale into insignificance beside him, although now she studied it more closely she could see his face was too strongly defined for classical beauty and possibly too rugged for a lot of women to find handsome.

So where did the sex appeal—the magnetism—stem from? Good looks? A great body? Well, she didn't know anything about his body apart from the fact that it filled a well-tailored three-piece suit very nicely. A combination of physical attributes and some inner fire?

'I'm sorry. Did I fall asleep on you? How rude of me. It's something I trained myself to do in boring university lectures and I've kept the practice going as it's useful from time to time in hospital meetings.'

He smiled disarmingly—and tiredly—at her.

'And when women prattle on about their work,' she added, returning his smile but cautiously. 'Come along, I'll drop you back at your hotel.'

She stood up as she spoke and watched him rise, then stretch some stiffness out of his back.

It was a homely picture, a man stretching tiredly in her kitchen. Her father had often done it, before walking up the stairs to bed.

Shutting the thought of men and beds away, she led him into the hall, towards the outer door, not the stairway.

'I could walk,' he said, catching up with her, moving with her so their bodies all but brushed together.

'I'll drive you,' she said firmly, 'then phone you in the morning to tell you what I've arranged with the obstetrician. I'll also follow up on the agencies who could provide support for Lucia's journey home.'

He hesitated at that, then thanked her, again opening her car door, holding it while she got in and shutting it with firmness but no bang.

'Was Lucia right about you having time off in the near future?' he asked. 'Would it be so impossible for you to accompany her home? We would pay your fare and for your time, of course.'

The questions were so unexpected it took a moment for Paige to absorb them.

'You said yourself, or intimated, that it will be a hellish journey,' she pointed out. 'The pair of them either weeping—or—worse still, I suspect—smooching for the entire journey.'

'Smooching? I don't know the word.'

She was glad of the darkness within her small sedan for her cheeks had scorched again.

'Kissing and cuddling,' she said stiffly. 'It's probably a slang expression.'

'Ah!'

He seemed to ponder it for a moment, then returned to his original question.

'But you do have holidays? You would have the time to undertake the journey?'

'You're a persistent cuss!' she muttered at him. 'And before you ask what a cuss is, I'll tell you. It's a slang word for a person, nothing derogatory.'

'I am glad of that,' he said gravely but she didn't need to see his lips to know his smile was back in place. 'Well?'

'I suppose the answer is yes as far as time is concerned,' she admitted slowly, trying to ignore an excited voice that was yelling at her to stop arguing. No need to tell him that she'd already considered taking Lucia home—would possibly have offered if he'd phoned instead of coming so unexpectedly. Once she'd returned Lucia to the bosom of her family, she could explore Italy, perhaps go across to France, visit Paris, see something of the world as she'd intended doing before James had come along.

So why wasn't she responding more positively now he'd suggested it? Because he'd suggested it?

She pulled up in front of the hotel and turned to the visitor.

'But I don't think I want the job. In fact, I couldn't do it as a job. Lucia is a friend. If I went, I would pay my own fare.'

He shifted slightly in his seat, turning to face her.

'I would like you to consider it, Paige Morgan,' he said, ignoring her proviso, 'if only for Lucia's sake. You must have learned how volatile she is. If a nurse she did not like were to accompany her, do you think she would obey her?'

'That's moral blackmail. I can arrange for her to meet the nurse before she's due to travel—to meet several and make the choice herself.'

He smiled as if he'd won which was strange considering she thought her own argument had been the winning one, then he opened the car door and swung his legs out, turning back to say, 'Thank you for everything, from taking such care of Lucia to your company this evening and the tasks you are still undertaking for us. I shall look forward to speaking with you in the morning.'

The words were formally delivered, and the hand he offered to her was for a shake goodnight, nothing more. Paige took it, shook it and this time withdrew her own before it could be enticed to linger.

'Goodnight,' she responded, an echo in her mind, something from schooldays, adding a silent 'sweet prince'.

But there was nothing 'sweet' about the princely tactics, she realised a few days later. The humbled and repentant groom had arrived and, as Marco had predicted, had wept all over his errant bride. He'd cried for joy about the pregnancy and groaned for Lucia's pain every time Paige tested her blood or injected insulin.

'You should be learning to do this for her or insisting she do it herself,' Paige told him crossly late one afternoon when her patience had worn thin and she'd decided she had to get rid of them, even if it meant driving them to Sydney and putting them on the plane herself.

'Marco's getting a nurse for me when I go home so Alex does not need to know,' Lucia told her with a sly smile. 'Marco promised me before he left. But I think you will have to come home with me, Paige, for the nurses you are finding are not good, not—what is your word, compatible?'

'You don't have to be compatible with someone who checks your diet, tests your blood and injects insulin,'

Paige stormed. 'Whether you like the person or not, all you have to do is grin and bear it!'

The pretty lips moved into pout position.

'I will not have people near me who upset me. Dr Edgar told me that being emotional is bad for me and the baby, and how can I not be emotional if some stranger I do not like is pricking me?'

Paige sighed and shook her head, wishing Dr Edgar had told Marco the same thing. This disapproval of the available nurses was the thin edge of the wedge—a move she should have seen coming from the moment his highness had agreed to her agency suggestion with such docility. He probably knew his sister well enough to guess her reaction to being thwarted.

His phone call followed so promptly on their conversation that she wondered if Lucia had sent some message winging through space. Not that he didn't call regularly—usually speaking to her as well as to Lucia, often talking for an hour or more as if they were friends, not casual acquaintances.

'Lucia mentioned again that you have time off from your work,' he began when they'd exchanged the usual civilities and established he wanted to speak to her, not Lucia. 'Are you not well that you need a long break? Or do you have family affairs to settle? Some personal reason for taking this time off from a job you obviously enjoy?'

He sounded concerned for her, which was nice even if there was no need, but how could she explain why she was leaving a job that had come to mean so much to her. It was something she found hard to explain even to herself. She pretended it was partly because she'd worked without a break for four years, right through her relationship with James and its traumatic conclusion, determined not to let down the people she'd committed herself to serve, but deep down she knew it was more than that.

'It's more for business reasons,' she began, then wondered why she was explaining anything to this man. It was certainly nothing to do with him.

'Personal business?' he probed.

'No, it's connected to the running of the service.' He'd irritated her and she snapped the words at him.

He said in a sympathetic voice, 'Ah, it became too much for you.'

She realised she'd have to take it further, although she'd never voiced the inner uncertainties which had prompted her to make this move.

'It did not become too much for me,' she retorted, then weakened enough to admit, 'although I do need some time off. But I began to realise that it was wrong for such a diverse service to rely so heavily on the knowledge and experience of just one person.'

She hesitated, not sure if he would understand what she was trying to say, not sure why she wanted him to!

'It was probably limiting its growth as well because all it had was my vision of it. Anyway, we'd already formed a committee which now administers the government-allocated funds, and when I spoke to the committee members about my reservations they agreed and have appointed two women to take my place. It's a trial of sorts—for a few months to begin with. It's job-sharing for the appointees, but for the service it means two new people coming to it with fresh ideas.'

There was no need to add that if the trial did work she'd be unemployed. Footloose and fancy-free. Which she *thought* was what she wanted.

'It might also benefit the people who use it because it

is not good for anyone to become too reliant on any one particular person.'

His comment told her he did understand and she smiled.

'That's what I keep telling Lucia.'

'Ah, but that is different, for you would be doing her and her family a very great favour if you accompanied her to Italy. And, with the service in good hands, you could be our guest for some time. It would be my pleasure to show you something of my country.'

'I thought you worked!' she replied. '"Prince" is a title, not a job description, you said. No doctor I know has enough free time to be running a tourist around the place.'

He didn't argue but she heard a ripple of laughter echo through the phone, felt her body respond to it and reminded herself how foolish it would be to expose her hormones to him again. The phone calls were bad enough—especially as she now looked forward to them and felt flat and disappointed when he didn't phone.

Not that they spoke of personal matters or exchanged confidences. Conversations tended to be more work—or Lucia—oriented. Like tonight, when his next question was about Mrs Bevan.

'Her sister has come to live with her,' Paige told him. 'I'm so pleased for both of them as it's an ideal arrangement.'

'One you could not have organised better yourself?' he teased, and again she felt a rush of warmth, as if the conversation *was* more personal.

They said goodbye with no more mention of Lucia or the logistics of her journey home, but as Paige put down the receiver and began to prepare their evening meal she could hear the sound of his amusement lingering in her ears and imagine how his face had looked when he'd laughed.

It wasn't until she'd peeled the same carrot four times that she realised her mind wasn't on the job—and what was left of the carrot was inedible!

Without a doubt, the man had a most unsettling influence on her, and no matter how much part of her wanted to give in to Lucia's wiles, she knew she was better off with many thousands of kilometres and an ocean between herself and Marco Alberici.

It was a distance which was growing smaller with every second they spent on the plane, the ocean crossed so effortlessly it might as well not have existed. Although just how she came to be sitting in the first-class section of the huge jetliner—just *when* she'd given in—she wasn't entirely certain.

'Only one more hour and we will be in Rome!' Lucia said, her face radiant as she slipped into the empty seat beside Paige and snuggled down next to her. 'Silly Alex is asleep, but I am too excited. You are excited, Paige?'

'I suppose so,' Paige agreed, not adding that she was even more relieved. The task of keeping Lucia stable had been more difficult than she'd imagined, and she'd be thankful to get her patient back down to earth and delivered into the hands of whoever would monitor the rest of her pregnancy.

'Do you think my mother will come to Rome to meet us, or will Marco arrange a car and driver to collect us and make Mama wait at home?'

'I've no idea,' Paige told, pleased that Marco meeting them in person wasn't listed as a possibility. She began to wonder if she could hand Lucia over and leave immediately—well, she'd have to run through the regimen Lucia was on, but as soon as she'd done that…

However, it was Marco she saw as she wheeled her suitcase out of customs, although Lucia hadn't spotted him, running instead to a slight attractive woman who stood a little to the right of him.

'We will travel north in two cars,' he announced, after shaking Paige's hand in welcome and taking her case from her suddenly nerveless fingers. 'Lucia will wish to chatter to her mother and Alex will doubtless want to stay with her, so I will take you.'

'But Lucia—she's still my patient, I assume. Shouldn't I stay with her?'

He smiled, ignored her objection and introduced her to his mother who was voluble in her praise—and as fluent in English as her son and daughter.

'You will go with Marco in his car.' The older woman repeated Marco's plans. 'And worry no more about Lucia for we have a niece of mine, a nurse, who will care for Lucia. She is older than Lucia—with two nearly grown-up sons—but she had the same problem in her pregnancies so knows exactly what to do for Lucia. She is in the car, awaiting us, and as the journey is only a short few hours she can watch Lucia as we travel while you begin a holiday. You will see something of our country as Lucia was seeing yours before she became ill.'

It seemed a strange way of looking at the runaway bride scenario, Paige thought, smiling to herself as Lucia's mother proceeded to bustle them out of the airport and into cars.

'She amuses you, my mother?' Marco asked as he lifted her suitcase into the boot.

'No, of course not but, seeing her in action, it's obvious where you and Lucia get your organising ability.'

He stepped towards her, grave, not smiling.

'We have organised you too much? Persuaded you against your will?'

Paige shrugged. Now she was actually here, within range of whatever it was that attracted her to him, she remembered why she hadn't wanted to come. But, to be honest, since she'd said finally given in to the combined pleas of Marco, Lucia and Alex, a very real excitement had been building within her.

And she should admit it. She sniffed the air—kerosene fumes, like any other airport—but couldn't she smell a hint of Rome as well?

'No, I'm happy to be here,' she told him. 'It's just strange to be transported to a place that's been a familiar name for as long as I can remember.'

'Roma! Rome, as you call it.' His eyes looked deep into hers for a moment. 'It will be my privilege to show it to you, but first we go to my home. Lucia has told you about it? It is a small place beyond Spoleto in Umbria, more a village that has grown too big to be a village yet not big enough to be a town in the real sense. In Umbria we have cheap power from the rivers so industry has grown up in the valleys near them. This has provided jobs, brought new people to the area.'

He hesitated and Paige had the impression that he'd been about to say something else—about either the people or the town—but he turned the conversation sideways, asking, 'Has Lucia talked much about it?'

'About Spoleto, which, I gather, is Alex's home,' Paige said. 'I looked it up in the atlas. It's up the Via Flamina, a town strategically placed to protect one of the great Roman ways.'

Marco seemed pleased but said nothing, merely opened the car door for her and waited until she was comfortable before closing it. The car smelt rich—leather seats, no doubt—and the wood panelling on the dashboard shone with a deep lustre. All of which distracted her from watching him as he walked around the bonnet, but when he slid in behind the wheel the car lost its sensory appeal, all her receptors being too occupied with the driver.

'It is not a great Roman way but a motorway on which we begin our journey. Like all cities, getting in and out is difficult. You will talk while I concentrate on the traffic. Tell me how the flight progressed, how Lucia's health is now.'

Paige should have objected to the peremptory tone but talking was probably a good idea. And looking around, even if it was only at an Italian motorway and Italian traffic, was an even better idea as Marco's body was like a magnet to her eyes and if she wasn't careful she'd be sitting and staring at him for the 'few short hours' it took to reach his home.

'The flight went better than I thought it would,' she admitted. 'I took a good supply of food in case we were delayed anywhere and I waited until Lucia's meals were served before giving her the quick-acting insulin. Funny things were different, though. Because of the pressurisation in the plane, you have to inject less air into the vials than usual before withdrawing the insulin. Small adaptations to be made.'

'But you handled them.' He sounded pleased by her competence, though he must have assumed it to entrust his sister to her care.

'I did—and even managed to persuade both Alex, who has no great taste for exercise either, and Lucia to walk around the interior of the airports where we had short fuel stops. That was another difference in the plane.

Although she did agree to do half an hour of walking around the cabin every six hours, the exercise had less effect on her glucose levels than a similar walk did at home.'

He glanced her way again and she could read his interest on his face.

'Something to do with different atmospheric conditions perhaps?'

He smiled and Paige's heart teetered on the brink of chaos, though there was no leap of imagination which could make talk of atmospheric conditions at all seductive!

'I guess so,' she managed. 'Or perhaps she needs more exercise at this stage. I've tried to tell her about the possibility of having a large baby and the importance of watching the weight she puts on, but exercise and Lucia?'

'A tough task,' he agreed, 'although now she is home perhaps she will swim. Nicolette, my cousin, will see she does whatever is necessary. Is Lucia aware she might need to have a Caesarean birth?'

That was better—medical matters could distract more of her attention from the company.

'Dr Edgar realised he wouldn't be treating her all through her confinement so I doubt he mentioned it. Mind you, with Lucia's obsession about not inflicting injury on her body, it might not be a bad idea to tell her of the possibility. It might make exercise seem more enticing.'

Marco chuckled, echoing the word 'enticing' in equally enticing tones, tilting Paige's mind back towards his physical appeal.

'And her blood glucose? It's holding down at reasonable levels?'

That told her where his mind was centred, and that any

physical sensations she might be experiencing were definitely one-sided. Yet when they'd spoken on the phone those nights his interest had often veered towards the personal, his desire for her to undertake the journey seemingly centred on more than concern for Lucia's health.

Or had she read more into his words than he'd intended? Allowed herself to drift into a fairytale again...

She sighed inwardly, and tried to dredge up some enthusiasm for this technical discussion of Lucia's health.

'Between four and eight—though more often close to eight. I've been afraid to raise the insulin level too quickly in case she began to suffer hypos. In the beginning she was very unstable, but by the time we left Dr Edgar seemed content with the way the pregnancy is progressing and the scans show no sign of distress in, or damage to, the foetus.'

A car shot past her window, frightening her with its speed and sudden appearance. Of course, she'd have to rethink the traffic conditions in view of the left-hand driving—would she drive her herself, perhaps hire a car? What plans had the family made? And should she go along with them or obey the dictates of common sense and remove herself from his home as fast as possible?

She glanced at Marco who was concentrating on the road, his long slender fingers resting lightly on the steering wheel. Get out, her head replied to the unasked question. A.S.A.P. But the yearning inside her heart suggested a different answer. She looked away before her eyes could be tempted to study his face in more detail, determine why the combination of his features provided such potency, and stared out the window where another feeder lane was pouring more traffic onto the concrete ribbon of road.

'Does your cousin speak English or should I write down the routine I've been following with Lucia and get you to translate it for her?'

She felt his movement and turned as he looked towards her—and smiled.

'The perfect nurse,' he teased. 'Always thinking of the patient.'

She held her body very still as she dealt with the shock waves of that smile.

'Yes, she speaks English. My grandmother—and hers—was English so we all visited England often and learned from her when we were children. In fact, we had an English nanny for a while who also taught us at home until my father decided we should attend the local school. My older sisters and I, that is. Lucia was a late baby— which might explain why she has been perhaps more pampered than the rest of us and is now not so independent.'

'Not so independent?' Paige repeated. 'That's the understatement of the year!'

'She has been a trial to you,' he said, those deep dark tones of empathy reverberating in his voice and crawling across her already exacerbated nerves. 'I am sorry.'

'She hasn't been that bad,' Paige responded and she knew the words sounded weak enough for him to disbelieve them where, in truth, the weakness had another source. Himself!

They were off the motorway now, travelling through country so green it seemed to shimmer in the warmth of the sun. A mountain range rose to one side of them, snow sprinkled like talcum powder on the topmost peaks. Every hill, it seemed, had either the battlements of an old fortified castle on the top of it or a village clinging to its slopes. In her mind Umbria had been the colour so close to it in name, a sandy brown, taupe, golden even—sun-burnt, like parts of Australia. But this land was green—grey-green where olive trees marched up the slopes, lush emerald in the meadows where poppies and some yellow flower she couldn't identify grew wild.

And the stones of the old buildings were white or pink, the colours muted by age but warm, inviting—welcoming. Marco was forgotten—well, almost forgotten—as she relaxed back into the seat and let these first visual impressions of this foreign land flood her senses.

Marco smiled to himself as he glanced at his guest. So, the magic was working on her. He'd often wondered how other people saw his country—whether they felt the physical renewal which came over him as he drove through the countryside after even a short absence. Today he'd deliberately chosen the longer way home, taken a smaller road which led through villages and wound along the valley beneath the Sibilline range.

Originally, he'd thought it would give him time to broach the subject of the job he wanted her to do, but now she was here he was uncertain about it. Not so much about the task he wished her to undertake for him, but about having this woman in his home for any length of time. She intrigued him, fascinated him—attracted him, if the truth be told—but instinct told him she wasn't a woman with whom one could carry on a light-hearted affair then say goodbye without regrets.

This was a love-and-marriage type of woman, and his own family history had proved that marrying outside one's own nationality—even province, his mother said—was fraught with danger.

'Oh, Marco, it is beautiful!'

She turned towards him, her cheeks flushed and her eyes bright with pleasure, breathing the words in a tone of such wonder he was tempted to forget the danger, stop the car and cover those soft lips with his.

'Not what you expected?' he asked instead, absurdly pleased by her pleasure.

'Not at all,' she said, smiling at him, the rose colour deepening in her cheeks and the green of her eyes matching the grass beyond the windows.

He breathed deeply, reminded himself that driving along narrow winding roads required all of his attention and began to play the host.

'That high peak is Mt Sibillini, the cluster of mountains called the Sibillini range although they are part of the Apennine range which forms the backbone of Italy.'

Did he sound like a tour guide? Most likely, but that was too bad. It was better than sounding like a lover!

'The river is the Tessino and we follow its valley to Spoleto and beyond that town to my home. Spoleto is a very old town. It was very conscious of its importance in Roman times, and people from Spoleto thought themselves immensely superior to those of Perugia and Assisi.'

He glanced towards his guest and saw a smile make tiny creases in her cheeks. He guessed what she was thinking!

'I am not of Spoleto but a village beyond it,' he reminded her. 'Different situation altogether.'

She turned towards him and he saw the whole smile instead of just a part of it.

'Oh, I'm sure of that,' she replied with mocking gravity, although the glint of gold in her eyes told of silent laughter.

'Well, it is!' he said, a little piqued but pleased as well that they could enjoy a joke together.

'See that red tiled building beyond the grove of olive

trees?' he said as they drew closer to the new village. 'That is the factory, the *fabbrica,* my grandfather built after the Second World War. He was careful to site it so it did not stand out too much and design it so it looked like a farm complex, not a factory.'

'It certainly doesn't yell "industrial area" as you drive past, which so many of our factory complexes do,' Paige agreed, studying the area as they travelled slowly by, then turning her head towards him. 'Lucia told me your father died some years ago. Are you involved with the running of the factory?'

'Not in any administrative capacity, although all the family members are on the board. One of my sisters runs the place now, and does an excellent job. It was she who inherited the family's business acumen and we all acknowledge how fortunate we are to have her.'

Paige chuckled, a sound that reminded him of the sound of a spring on the hill above his home.

'That doesn't sound at all like my preconceived notion of an Italian man speaking. For some reason, the image is always of the "bed and kitchen" breed.'

'Bed and kitchen?' he teased, wanting to see the colour deepen in her cheeks. 'A woman's place is in the home— that kind of thing? Yes, we do tend to think in stereotypes of different nationalities. You weren't my idea of a sun-bronzed Aussie.'

She laughed again, and the colour did chase across her cheeks. Alluring. Intoxicating.

Dangerous!

'So we're even,' she declared. 'Tell me about the factory your sister runs so well.'

He talked about it, about the footwear they manufactured, mostly school shoes and children's shoes, about the competition from the American-style 'labels' and

keeping abreast of current trends. He could feel his body
relaxing now they were close to home, now his guest was
less tense and more aware of her surroundings—admiring
them, excited by the beauty.

Perhaps he should let his little corner of Italy work its
magic before mentioning the project. Yes, he could spare
an extra few days to show her around, take her to Assisi
and Norcia, perhaps up the mountains for a night, then
broach the subject when she was hooked on Italy—
hooked enough to want to stay a while.

CHAPTER SIX

'YOUR house?'

Paige whispered the words, awed by the beauty of the surroundings and by the sight of the modern house built to blend with the natural landscape yet take advantage of the views of the mountains and deep cleft of the valley.

'You're surprised?'

She glanced at Marco, saw the smile on his lips and read his love for his home in the way he looked ahead.

'Well, we've driven past enough old castles for me to wonder if perhaps they were all inhabited by princes, dukes, counts and other titled gents, but this, it's breath-taking—the view, the way the house nestles into the hill as if it's part of it.'

'Much of it is,' he told her, stopping the car on a wide sweep of gravelled drive in front of shallow stone steps which led up to a long, sun-washed terrace. 'The structure of the old house was weakened in an earthquake, and our local engineers and architects now tie the houses more firmly to the ground, although still allowing for flexibility so walls will sway rather than crack. We have used more timber than many Italian houses for that same reason, but tried to keep the ambience of our old home.'

He fell silent after this explanation but remained in the car, and she sensed he wanted her to take it all in—to like his house, in fact.

'The view helps,' she said, turning once again towards the range of mountains, yet knowing that from the terrace she would see down the valley over which the house stood guard and the village they'd passed only minutes earlier, a tumble of old houses, the mountain road widening to a piazza between the shops and cafés, then narrowing again, twisting once more before reaching this point. And beyond that, the newer village near the factory. Or would it be invisible from up here?

'It *is* special,' he agreed, and now he did get out, walking around the car to open her door then leading her up the steps and along the terrace to the far end, where she could see not only down the valley but higher up to where water tumbled down the rocky cleft, the sound of it reaching her ears like the distant notes of a familiar melody.

'Welcome to my home,' he said with great formality, and she sensed that was how it was to be between them and was thankful. Well, she told herself she was thankful because 'formal' would provide a mask behind which she could safely hide her attraction to him. But there was disappointment present as well, like the momentary sense of regret on waking from a pleasant dream, an illusion pricked as easily as a bright-coloured bubble.

'Thank you,' she said, shutting the book on the fairy-tale and deciding to make the most of the short stay she would have in this magical place. She walked back towards the car, knowing he'd flipped a switch which had released the lock on the boot before getting out. She'd get her case, show him she didn't need his little courtesies—didn't want them as they confused her already overreacting body into thinking things it shouldn't.

'I will see to your case, but first you must come inside, walk through the house with me so you know your way around and feel at home in it.'

Which is the very last thing I want to feel, she mused.

But she couldn't argue with her host who was only being polite—and formal!

He took her elbow and steered her towards a wooden door which was already open as if to welcome its master. The ochre-coloured tiles which paved the terrace continued inside, leading into a massive front hall. In the very centre was a square carpet, brightly woven in green and blue, and on it a table which held, beside an arrangement of wild poppies interspersed with what looked like grass and wheat, a jumble of mail, a woman's hat and a child's ragged doll.

It was homely, she realised, in spite of the formidable size—the little bits of untidiness not detracting from the perfection of the entry but adding warmth to it.

'This is the vestibule.' Marco pointed out the obvious, then waved his hand to indicate direction. 'On the right we have the living room, then dining room, all open space because the old house had small rooms and my mother wanted space around her. These rooms lead onto the terrace, while on the left my study and the kitchen open out to the garden and pool area.'

They looked into all the rooms, before crossing the entry to stairs which gave the appearance of being suspended in space.

'Upstairs are bedrooms and bathrooms and beyond them, on that level, one of my sisters has an apartment, then above that on the next level there are rooms for guests where Lucia and Alex will stay while Nicolette learns from you about Lucia's care.'

Paige shook her head.

'You've lost me. Do all these people come in and out through here?'

He smiled at the question and led her up the stairs.

'You will understand the levels when you see them.

All are connected through hallways and the outer terraces but within themselves they are private and self-contained. They are also accessible from the road which goes beyond where we stopped—in fact, to the very top of the mountain.'

'So, it's three houses in one,' she said, hoping she wasn't showing open-mouthed astonishment at the bedroom Marco had entered.

'Four, actually, because my mother's quarters, beyond the kitchen, are also self-contained, although she and I share one cook and gardener and usually eat together in the main dining room. Tonight you will meet us all for, with Lucia's return, the family will gather. This room will suit you?'

She looked at the solid four-poster bed with its net of brilliant white, its snowy embroidered quilt and lace-trimmed pillows. She bit back a comment that it looked too bridal, flushed at the thought and turned hurriedly towards the windows.

'It's unbelievable,' she murmured, forcing out the words through lips which had become uncomfortably dry. It was the bed, and errant images superimposed on it which had caused the trouble. And Marco standing there—so at ease in his own territory it added an extra dimension to his attraction.

'I'm glad you are pleased,' he said, coming closer to peer over her shoulder as if to check the view was still where it should be. 'I would like you to be happy here.'

The sentence jarred—or was it something in his voice which put her senses on alert? Yet there'd been sincerity in the remark as well, and that deserved a truthful answer.

'It would be hard not to be,' she said. 'Such comfort and such beauty. But I won't stay long. Your family has had enough disruption recently with Lucia's disappearance, then coping with the knowledge of her condition. Once I've explained things to Nicolette I'll be on my way. I've made some plans to travel now that I'm over here.'

It wasn't quite a lie, as she did plan to travel, although where and when and for how long she'd been unable to decide—her mind refusing to tackle the multitude of choices Europe offered the first-time visitor.

When he didn't reply she turned and looked at him, catching a slight frown, quickly erased, between his eyebrows.

'Of course, it is up to you, but I have free time now the conference is over. I was hoping to show you what this area has to offer. It is not as well known to tourists as Tuscany, although in my mind it has as much beauty and antiquity.'

Another warning sounded inside her head, but all the man was offering was simple kindness born of a desire that others might appreciate the attractions of the country he loved. She'd done the same herself, driving Lucia on weekends to the national parks near her home town, showing her the rugged beauty of the landscape, the chasms down which wild waters plunged and roared.

'That's very kind,' Paige answered, trying for a formality to match his earlier behaviour. 'Now, perhaps I should unpack then see if the other car has arrived. The sooner I can talk to Nicolette, the sooner we can get Lucia settled between us.'

'You should rest, not concern yourself about Lucia,' he chided, standing far too close and showing no inclination to take the hint and fetch her suitcase from the car.

'I'm far too hyped-up to rest, although a shower would be nice.' She'd get the case herself—after all, it was what she'd intended doing. But even when she walked towards the door Marco remained where he was by the window, staring, not at the view but at her, as if confused by who she was or what she was doing in his house.

'I'm sorry.' He came to with an almost visible start. 'Aldo should by now have brought your case inside. No doubt it is in the hall.' He was all business again, but the look she'd seen in his eyes a second earlier had been personal—almost sexual in its appraisal—as if his thoughts had strayed a long way from formality.

He'd have to stop thinking about her as a woman—consider her as a colleague, nothing more. Or perhaps a friend of Lucia's. He'd handled dozens of the pretty young things honing their flirting skills on a safe 'big brother' figure. Not that Paige Morgan could be classed as a 'pretty young thing'—she was attractive more than pretty, but it was her colouring that fascinated him—the pale rose of her lips, the way a darker shade of that same colour washed her cheeks, the gold-flecked green eyes and shiny, silken hair.

Nor had she had done any flirting. Had that added to his interest in her physical charms—the casual indifference with which she treated him?

He found her suitcase outside the door and carried it into the room, lifting it onto the low table at the end of the bed. And he'd better keep out of this room, for the vision he'd had earlier of corn-coloured hair spread across those white pillows had seriously threatened his intention to treat her formally.

'I will be downstairs. A light luncheon will be served at one, but if you are tired and wish to sleep, Mirelle will fix you something to eat later in the afternoon.'

She smiled at him, which made him forget the formality decision once again.

'I understand the rule with international travel is to try to get into step with the new time zone as soon as possible so, inviting though that bed looks, I won't sleep until later.'

'Perhaps after lunch,' he replied. 'That would be falling into the natural rhythms of this country for we still follow the custom of the long lunch.'

'You sleep after lunch?' she challenged, her eyes glinting with a teasing mischief.

'I rest and read, perhaps do book-work. You will find all business stops here, even doctoring.'

'And surgery? Are patients scheduled around this long lunch?'

Her interest was apparent in her voice, and he hoped she would stay for he'd like to show her around the private hospital in Terni where he had worked for many years. Still could work in the future, if everything else fell into place.

'Like travellers avoiding jet lag, we try to keep our hospital routines as much as possible in keeping with the patients' natural way of life, although, like all such places, they are woken early by the business of the day. So, yes, in many hospitals we take two or even three hours off at lunchtime, although when the theatres are busy patients are scheduled right through this time to maximise use of the facilities.'

Paige listened to his voice—heard the words and stored away the information—but it was the lilting cadences which held her, the slightly different intonations and phrasing, like music that is unfamiliar yet intensely pleasing to the ear.

'I'd like to see an Italian hospital,' she heard herself say, and knew immediately it was a tactical error because it was committing her to stay beyond the strict limit of the time needed for handing over Lucia's supervision, prolonging her stay within the range of the spell this man could so effortlessly cast about her body. 'I might do that later when I'm in Rome,' she added in a desperate attempt to regroup.

'Are you in such a hurry you must rush away from here?' Marco replied. 'Is there someone awaiting your return? A lover perhaps?'

Surprise made her flick her eyes to his. She saw a confusion there which equalled her own. He hadn't meant to say that. Looked remorseful. Perhaps Lucia had told him of James and he was sorry for her. Well, she didn't want his sympathy.

Just his body, a teasing voice whispered in her head.

She hid a rueful smile and turned her attention to her suitcase, unzipping it, pretending she wasn't perturbed at all.

'I'm in no hurry,' she said airily, 'but I won't trespass on your family's good nature for too long.' Now she looked at him and let him see the smile. 'I may not be a sun-bronzed Aussie, but I'm an independent one.'

He returned her smile with a devastating one of his own.

'That's offering me a challenge, Paige Morgan. I shall have to see what I can do to change your mind.'

And on that cryptic note he walked from the room, leaving Paige to stare after him, her mind telling her body he hadn't meant it the way he'd made it sound—or the way she'd wanted it to sound.

She showered and debated what one wore to a family lunch in Italy. Not jeans, she decided, selecting a long, button-through linen skirt the colour of ripe wheat and teaming it with a paler yellow blouse. At lunch she would sit beside Nicolette and explain Lucia's routine, after which she would no longer feel obliged to stay.

Politeness decreed she remain at least one night—possibly two—but no more.

'You will sit here, by Marco, as you are our honoured guest.' His mother took up the decreeing, less than an hour later. Knowing Lucia needed insulin before the meal, Paige had gone down to the big room early and had found the cousin waiting for her there. They had talked of Lucia's case and of Nicolette's own experiences with pregnancy and diabetes.

'You'll be far better qualified to help than I was,' Paige had told her, and the older woman had smiled as if pleased by the remark.

'Although I doubt she will mind me as well as she must have minded you,' she'd said, which had made Paige laugh.

'Lucia minding anyone would be a sight to see,' she'd answered. 'I found the only thing that worked was threats about losing her figure.'

'Marco told me you tried that. Yes, I can see it would work.'

The talk had become more technical, Nicolette explaining that her aunt had already arranged for an obstetrician to see Lucia and asking Paige to accompany them on their first visit the following day.

'I have read the letter Lucia brought from her doctor, and Lucia has talked of her routine. I have insulin here, but if you have brought some with you...'

She paused, as if uncertain where to draw the line between her tasks and Paige's, and Paige hastened to assure her that she could take over immediately.

'Although I'm happy to discuss anything with you if you feel at all concerned.' She held up the small case she'd carried with her on the plane. 'This is my supply of drugs. I should transfer it to the refrigerator.'

Nicolette showed her to the kitchen, where they continued their conversation, although it was carried on with difficulty as the woman preparing the meal in the kitchen, introduced as Mirelle, asked questions of Nicolette and tutted over the answers she was given, throwing up her hands and evidently praising God for either Lucia's return to the family or the news that a new baby was on the way.

The next interruption was Lucia herself, who submitted to hugs and what seemed like loud recriminations of her behaviour from Mirelle, who promptly burst into tears when Paige slid the injection under the skin of Lucia's abdomen.

'We'll talk later,' Nicolette suggested. 'Far too much commotion going on here.'

At that stage Signora Alberici had arrived on the scene, sweeping them all out of the kitchen and into the dining room.

'Nicolette, you will sit by Lucia, with Alex between you and Miss Morgan.' Signora Alberici continued her arrangements. 'I shall take my place on Marco's left and there will be no talk of Lucia's illness or condition at this table. After we have rested, Nicolette and Miss Morgan can confer again.'

Paige hid a smile—well, it was hidden until she glanced at Marco and he winked at her.

'Miss Morgan thinks Lucia and I get our organising ability from you,' he teased his mother.

'Miss Morgan is too formal,' Paige protested, trying to cover what might seem like rudeness to the older woman. 'Please, call me by my first name, Paige.'

'It is an attractive name. It is often used in your family?'

It was an innocent query, but somehow, as lunch progressed, Paige realised that Marco's mother was not only a good organiser but was also adept at wheedling information out of her guests. The family now knew of her mother's early death, her upbringing by her adored father, the reasons for her decision to nurse rather than practise medicine as he had—most of the details of her life, in fact, apart from James!

'You will want to lie down, tired from all that questioning?' Marco asked as they left the dining room after a lunch which had offered an array of meats, salads, breads and luscious cheeses.

'I need exercise more than a rest,' Paige told him. 'I've eaten more than I do in a week and, to top it off, had wine at lunchtime! May I walk on up the road to the top of the hill?'

He smiled at her.

'You may do whatever you wish, Paige, for we would like you to treat this house as your own.' Once again he hesitated, then he smiled, triggering the sweep of sensory responses Paige had hoped she'd had under control. 'But the road is a dull walk on such a nice day. I know a better one through the fields if you could bear my company.'

'Typical Alberici way of putting something,' Paige scolded. 'If I say no, it will sound as if your company is insupportable. Lucia would do the same thing to me. You're all too good at painting people into corners.'

His smile widened, lit his eyes and twinkled down at her, sending heat coursing through her blood.

'So you do not find my company insupportable?'

'Not *all* the time,' she told him, wondering why she'd

let herself be drawn into this conversation. She should have said she was going to rest, or that she wanted to be on her own while she walked. But neither answer would have been true. The part of her which advocated half a loaf was better than no bread was clamouring to walk the mountain fields with him—though she guessed he wouldn't take kindly to being compared to bread.

'Shall we go?'

She shrugged, trying for casual and missing by a mile, especially when he led her to a hat stand in the front hall and chose a wide-brimmed raffia hat.

'It is a new one—my mother keeps a couple here for guests such as yourself, a gift from Casa Alberici.' He came towards her and set the hat on her head, standing so close she could see the rise and fall of his chest through the grey silky-knit shirt he was wearing. She felt the hat settle on her head, then the warmth of his fingers brushing her cheek as he tucked away a stray strand of hair.

'You improve the hat's beauty,' he said softly, and her body forgot all her mind's warnings about this man and went through a melting routine so unfamiliar she wondered if she might be sickening for something.

Or perhaps jet lag had symptoms like this. She *should* have rested!

'Come!'

He spoke softly, took her hand—that handholding thing again—and led her out the front door, taking the road for about twenty yards then heading off it to the right along a path towards a small stream which gurgled over satiny rocks.

'I must be back to speak to Nicolette when Lucia's blood test is due,' she said, forcing her mind from handholding and hot blood. She told herself it was a local custom and meant nothing to him.

'I shall have you back in time,' Marco promised, then he pointed to a peak and gave its name, taking his role as a guide seriously.

They crossed the stream, his hand providing support, but ahead the path narrowed and she was relieved to find they had to walk in single file—and, in order to do that, not hold hands.

But the thankfulness didn't last long for now she walked behind him, her eyes drawn to the way he moved, to shoulders wide enough to hold the world—although that was Greek legend, wasn't it—not fairytales?

'So, from my mother's probing, I gather the house I thought was owned perhaps by the government or some agency is, in fact, yours,' he said, when the ground flattened out and they could once again walk abreast.

Again that interest in her house. Well, it was far safer for her mind to puzzle over that than to think about his back and shoulders.

'Yes. It was too big for one person, and at the time I didn't want to sell it so I let the health service gradually take over most of the downstairs area.'

'Did you never think you'd have a family and need all those rooms?' he asked, and she hoped he hadn't seen her shiver.

'There's plenty of space for a family in the rest of the house. A formal living room and a conservatory which could be used as a dining room downstairs, plus four bedrooms and the small sitting room upstairs.'

He smiled at her.

'You sound defensive, Paige. Has someone, in the past, criticised your generosity in letting the service use the house, or do you sometimes wonder why you made such a splendid gesture? Do the people who fill your home aggravate you from time to time?'

She half smiled as she heard the echoes of James's outrage when she'd said she wanted to allow the community service to continue to operate there.

'But how can we entertain—have guests up from the city for weekends and functions—if your rabble is inhabiting half our house?' he'd said, and at that moment, well before she'd known about Gayle Sweeney, she'd wondered if marriage to James was really what she wanted.

'No, the people could never aggravate me,' she answered, tucking the memory back where it belonged—in the past.

'I thought not,' he said, and she caught a note of satisfaction in his voice, as if she'd confirmed some judgement he didn't mean to share with her.

They walked on again, the talk turning once again from work to the beauty of the countryside through which they strolled, although every now and then some comment made her realise that he was still thinking of the service—or the house from which it operated. In fact, the comments were so entwined she wondered if perhaps her brain was misbehaving—that she was imagining the double layering of the conversation.

'The Apennines run down the centre of Italy like a spine.' That was one example, for he followed it with a question unrelated to the view. 'Do you think people come because it *is* a house? Did you consider this in the early days, that, like the church hall proved too big for your playgroup, an office somewhere might have intimidated them and stopped the work before it began?'

Definitely not her imagination! She made the leap with

him, but *her* mind was on the beauty of the mountains which shed a kind of calm across her agitated soul.

'Yes, I think the house does make a difference. It's less formal so people feel more as if they're dropping in on a friend rather than consulting, in inverted commas. It's also geographically central to the poorer area of the town, which was another plus. If it was too much effort to get there, a large number of our clients wouldn't come.'

He seemed to consider this for a while, then nodded as if satisfied by the tenor of his thoughts—but kept them private, not speaking again until the full glory of the view was revealed.

'So, now we are on top of the world, as you see,' he said. They had reached the summit and serried rows of mountains marched across in front of them rising ever higher and higher towards the Alps, while below them, the valley lay spread like a multi-patterned and layered cloth beneath their feet.

'It's beautiful,' Paige breathed, turning slowly around through three hundred and sixty degrees to appreciate every angle of the magical view.

'Yes,' Marco responded, but his eyes were on her, not the view, and a huskiness in his voice made her heart flutter wildly. More jet lag—or perhaps altitude this time?

To cover her confusion, she bent and plucked a poppy, then another. With a small handful she straightened up to admire their fragile petals, and released them from suddenly nerveless fingers when Marco reached out for them.

She should walk away, look again at the mountains, start back down the track, but she couldn't move, held by some strange magic the place—or perhaps the company—had woven around her. He stepped closer, and she saw him lift his hand, felt the pressure as he tucked a poppy in her hat, then another and another.

'Very pretty,' he said, as if satisfied at what he'd done, but he didn't step away from her and her taut nerves screamed for release. She should have moved, but didn't. Instead she watched his hand rise again—one poppy left—and felt his fingers gently touch her skin as he tucked it, as red as blood, as bright as a flag of danger, into the opening of her shirt, the stem tickling at the cleft between her breasts, her body growing heavy with an aching need for more caresses.

'Beautiful,' he whispered, and this time she did move—stepping back, away from him, before he felt the tension of her need, the tightness of her nerves and flesh and sinews, the clammy heat which flooded through her body.

'Yes, it is,' she managed to say, pretending it was the view all the time which had interested him.

And perhaps it was. Perhaps to think anything else was to believe in fairytales.

CHAPTER SEVEN

WHICH could come true, Paige started to believe as the few days she'd intended staying slowly slipped into a week. She'd met Marco's other sisters, their husbands and the three small grandchildren that first evening. The chatter at the table, mostly in English for her benefit but with lapses into the musical beauty of Italian, had fascinated her. An only child of only children, she'd seen little of the interaction of an extended family, the warmth, support and security it offered, even when they were teasing each other or arguing volubly over their differences.

'And how you stayed sane with Lucia in your home for a whole month is beyond us all,' Paola exclaimed, when Paige had been drawn into telling how she'd met their sister.

The others agreed despite Lucia's protests and Alex's strong defence of his wife.

'I enjoyed having her stay with me,' Paige explained, but this, too, was howled down in disbelief and mirth.

'Unless you are a saint,' Anna, the younger, quieter sister suggested.

'Or a very special person,' Marco put in, and a certain huskiness in his voice made her shiver.

Thinking about that dinner party now, seven days later, Paige realised how often those words had repeated themselves in her head. Not that he'd meant them to be memorable, any more than he'd intended the glance he'd sent her way to carry a special message. But her silly heart had leapt with hope—only she hadn't realised it was hope until she'd analysed her feelings later. She'd assumed it was the same physical reaction he'd been causing since their first meeting.

Now, after a week spent mostly in his company, tasting wine in cellars tunnelled deep into the ground, climbing to the tops of peaks to breathe in the sharp cold air and dazzle the eyes with the beauty of the mountains, walking down the narrow, cobbled streets of tiny hill villages and standing on the ramparts of castles built as fortresses to withstand sieges in harsh and bloodier times, the hope had died, for there'd been no hint that the attraction she felt might be returned.

Although that wasn't entirely true. As they'd walked a wooded path at Monteluco, she'd seen a bird and had stopped suddenly, not wanting to frighten it away, and Marco had walked into her, taken her shoulders to steady himself and held her close for a moment. The tension in his body had communicated itself to her, and she'd half turned her head to see if she could guess what he was thinking and had caught a blaze of what had looked like desire flaring in his eyes.

Her breath held, Paige had waited, wanting the kiss his eyes were signalling, her body trembling with a need to be spun around and held against him so their shapes fitted and their bodies could feed each other's hunger.

But the blaze had died.

Quenched?

Or never there at all? A figment of her overactive imagination? Another fantasy?

Then at Assisi, late in the afternoon after the tourists had departed, they'd knelt in the tiny chapel where the gentlest of saints had died, and Marco had put his arm around her shoulders, a silent pledge of something she couldn't understand. Friendship perhaps, although her heart had whispered love, for in that sacred place there'd been no physical awareness—lust at bay for those precious moments.

However, apart from those two incidents, he'd become less personal in his attention, less likely to take her hand in his or slip flowers between her breasts.

Which made things worse for her, not better, for she, too, had stood apart and studied him—a prince who wasn't a prince—mixing and mingling with the local villagers, friends not subjects, all of whom treated him with both respect and camaraderie. He appeared to be an admirable man in every way, a pity when what she needed was something to dislike about him—a flaw to mar the image of perfection—at least one foot of clay!

'Today we will ''do'', as the tourists say, the new village and then enjoy a lunch in Spoleto,' he announced, meeting her at breakfast on the eighth day of her visit and bestowing on her a smile which made her mouth water.

'Surely you should be returning to work,' she argued. 'You've been very kind, but I'm beginning to feel guilty about taking up so much of your time. Not that I haven't enjoyed it, but I can't go on accepting your hospitality, doing nothing in return except disrupting your life.'

His smile slid off his face, then returned, a rueful version this time.

'Ah,' he said gravely, 'there's that, of course. But this morning it will be work for me. There are some people I must see in the new village and I thought it might interest you to accompany me. It is a situation not unlike the health service which operates from your home.'

She'd been standing by a laden sideboard, choosing fruit and crisp rolls for her breakfast—avoiding his smile, in fact—but something in his voice made her turn towards him. He sounded uncertain—which in Marco was extremely rare.

'It's a community service?'

He nodded and busied himself spreading honey on his roll. Avoiding an answer?

Intrigued, she crossed to the table and sat opposite him, nodded acceptance as he lifted the coffeepot and indicated her cup. She watched him pour her coffee, set the pot back on its heated pad in the centre of the table, then return his attention to his breakfast.

'And?'

He glanced up as if surprised by her question.

'And what?'

His face was still, his blue eyes deliberately masking any emotion.

'There's more, isn't there?' she persisted, and saw the eyes give way first, a gleam appearing fractionally before the smile.

'It doesn't work as we—or I—had hoped. I thought perhaps…' Not only uncertain but practically stuttering! Dithering!

Several pennies not only dropped but clanged, then echoed with reverberating force in her head, plunging her into such despair and uncertainty that she dropped her napkin on the table, stood up and left the room, crossing the big entry hall, heading for the terrace where the view of the mountain and the chuckle of the stream might offer solace to her wounded spirits.

Some hope! She paced the length of it, spun around to retrace her steps, trying to sort out the maelstrom of emotions bubbling and churning inside her. Marco had appeared by the door but he stopped there, not approaching, waiting for her to come to him. Which she didn't, turning short and pacing away from him.

'You are upset?' He put the obvious into words when she drew close a second time—near enough to hear his voice.

'Of course I'm upset!' she raged, flinging up her arms in a gesture which would do credit to any one of his volatile family. 'Why wouldn't I be upset?'

He approached her now, caution in every step he took, concern written clearly on his strong features.

'It is because I suggested you might like to see the health service?'

Now he sounded tentative, which *had* to be a con job. Tentative didn't feature in this man's genetic structure! Princes didn't come in tentative. Well, not the only one she knew!

She stared at him, thinking perhaps he was joking—that he must know how she was feeling.

'Because I said it wasn't running well?' he prompted, and as anger surged she felt her arms lift again.

'I don't give a damn about your service,' she stormed, 'or whether it's running well or not!' She about turned, pacing again, hoping the release of energy might loosen the knots in her intestines. Finding it didn't work as he caught up and paced beside her.

'But that was your intention all the time, wasn't it? And I should have known. Should have guessed when every second conversation was about my house and the way we'd set up our community service. I always found it strange, but did it click? Of course not. I'm too stupid!

'Not that I thought you'd phoned and talked to me, persuaded me to come for the sake of my flashing green eyes or outstanding beauty, but I thought it might be friendship! I let myself to think you were shunting me around the countryside because this imaginary friendship and your princely politeness decreed it, but you weren't, were you? You were softening me up—hoping I'd like the place, might be willing to stay a while and perhaps suggest something to help your ailing service. Was that the plot?'

She had read his thoughts—well, most of them—so accurately, Marco realised that whatever he wanted to say would now be tainted by her conclusions.

'I showed you my country with pride and love,' he said stiffly. 'I felt you would appreciate its special beauty and feel something of the pull it has for me.' He paused, feeling as shaken as if a layer of his soul had been stripped away. 'More than that, I did it in the hope that, in some small way, it might go towards a debt we can never repay—your loving care for, and attention to, Lucia. So gratitude played a part, but you are not the kind of person who accepts gratitude easily. You shrug our thanks aside, diminish what you did, which might make you feel comfortable but leaves us at a loss.'

'So, it's my fault now!' Paige retorted, reaching the end of the terrace and spinning around. He kept pace with her and as they turned he thought he read confusion in her lovely eyes. Instinct told Marco to take her in his arms until the confusion cleared, but fortunately his brain was still in partial working order and suggested he'd be compounding his mistake.

'No, there is no fault, I am simply talking. And, yes, even with so little experience of your service, I *was* impressed and I did wonder, if you agreed to accompany Lucia home, if you might have time to take a look at what we do and how we do it. I considered, with your experience, you might pick up on what we are doing wrong. Some things, I suspect, I have already learned, but fresh eyes could bring a new approach.'

She stopped pacing suddenly so he overshot her and

had to turn back to face her. Face eyes alive with anger and—disgust?

'Is the Machiavellian principle of weaving convoluted plans bred into all Italians?' she demanded. 'Did you have to do it this way? Why couldn't you have said, "Paige, I have a similar service in my home town and it isn't working. Would you be willing to take a look at it?" Would that have been so hard? Or would it have dented your pride to admit it wasn't working? You had to set me up like this? Hell's teeth, Prince Manipulator, if you'd asked I'd probably have said yes. *And* I could have claimed the cost of the trip off my tax!'

She stormed away from him again, leaving him wondering, not why he hadn't asked her outright but what on earth she meant by 'the cost of her trip'.

He asked when he caught up with her.

'I told you at the time that, if I were to take Lucia home it would be as a friend, not an employee—I *said* I would pay my own fare.'

It made no sense. Her anger must be making her irrational—and more attractive than he'd ever seen her, with the fire of her emotion flaming in her cheeks and sparkling in her eyes. Not that he would ever be able to admit that the green eyes might have played a part in all of this. Would he have worked so hard to persuade a woman less attractive to him to accompany Lucia?

'I could not countenance you undertaking a first-class journey at your own expense.' He managed to drag his disordered senses together enough to refute her foolish statement. 'I paid for all those tickets.'

'Checked your Visa account lately?' she shot back at him. 'Noticed a credit of one return first-class fare from Sydney to Rome?'

'You changed the tickets! Paid yourself! *Madonna*

mia!' He roared the accusation, the oath, at her, so hot with anger now himself he wondered he hadn't inflicted physical violence on her person.

Except to touch her—even in anger—was to invite trouble, for she affected his senses as no one ever had before, and he had to keep reminding himself that an affair wouldn't do for Paige Morgan. And anything more than an affair was so fraught with problems as to be impossible.

'Why shouldn't I?' she said pertly, and smiled because she knew, in forcing him to lose his temper, she'd won that duel.

'Because it is my responsibility to look after my family,' he pointed out, each word clipped and curt. 'Lucia is my responsibility and that was extended to you. I will not have you out of pocket because of the behaviour of my sister.'

Now she had to hide her smile.

'Can't do much about it, can you?' she sniped, then her smile faded as she added, 'And perhaps all this responsibility stuff has gone too far. Can't you see that's what has made Lucia the way she is? She's an adult. OK, a young adult at nineteen. But she's old enough to be taking responsibility for her own actions. Did you fuss over Anna and Paola in the same way, protect them from the world then thrust them into marriage with someone you'd chosen so that another dominant male could take responsibility for them?'

'I did not choose Alex for Lucia. It was not ''arranged'' so much as, my mother and his mother being friends, the two of them had grown to know each other.'

'Not good enough,' Paige struck back at him. 'You allowed the marriage to go ahead, knowing he was just as foolish as she was—and don't deny that because you told me so yourself!'

Her eyes challenged him but he could think of nothing in his own defence—except where his other sisters were concerned.

'Paola and Anna both chose their own husbands. They are women as independent as you yourself, university educated—which Lucia would have been if she hadn't gone her own headstrong way and insisted on marrying Alex the moment she was out of school.'

'Well, no one's going to change Lucia overnight, but you could start by stepping back and letting her and Alex make their own decisions. And, in future, think of me as one of your independent sisters, Marco, and don't take on responsibility for me, OK?'

She walked away, her pace now slowed, the movements of her body less stressed.

Enticing.

No, he could not be enticed by Paige! He'd listened to her talk about Australia, and had heard so much love in her voice at times he'd lost track of their conversation, distracted by the realisation that she felt as strongly about her homeland—even about her house—as he did about his. However much she exclaimed at or praised the beauty of his country, Australia would be tugging at her heart—as cool and misty England had beckoned to his grandmother.

It was a strange thought to be having at that moment, as most of his sexual thoughts concerning Paige Morgan had been halted by his certainty that she wasn't the type of woman to join him in a light-hearted but non-permanent affair. Permanent hadn't been an option before this morning.

Marco stared out towards the mountains and waited

for the beauty to work its magic and pacify his soul. Once upon a time that magic had worked on his body also, but since this woman with the hair like golden silk had come to stay, filling the empty corners of his house with her presence, his body had become immune to pacification, controlled only by the forceful exertions of his will-power, a lot of walking and the occasional cold shower.

Hardly appropriate at the moment!

What mattered now was to mend the rift between them. How?

What to say? To do?

How to repair the situation?

The mountains told him nothing. No oracles there to guide his way with cryptic comments.

He waited until Paige's path brought her close enough to hear his words, then said, 'You do not need to visit the service that concerns me. Or even visit Spoleto with me today. Anna is free and she has been wanting to take you to Gubbio, a favourite place of hers. Would you enjoy that?'

He'd almost added, Or would you prefer me to make arrangements for you to leave us? But the thought of her departure had become increasingly unsettling over the week she'd been with them, and he couldn't ask a question he didn't want her to answer.

'I haven't said I wouldn't see your service.'

The words flicked as sharp as stones against his already battered flesh.

'In fact, I'd be interested in it, *and* only too happy to make suggestions which might be worth a try, although I can't imagine I will be much help as an outsider, looking in. Perhaps Anna could take me there instead.'

It was the cruellest cut of all!

'You do not wish to see it with me?' The question

seemed to fly from his lips without forethought—instantly regretted as it sounded pathetic, like the cry of a child deprived of a treat.

She stared at him, her eyes assessing him as if weighing up his future trustworthiness.

'I'm still angry with you,' she warned, then she lifted her shoulders in a little gesture he'd come to know and watch for. 'But I suppose you'd be the best person to show me around.'

It was a truce of sorts—the best he could hope for at the moment.

'You should have something to eat,' he suggested, and a sidelong glance caught a smile flickering at the corner of her mouth.

'Is that damaging to your independence also?' he asked. 'Me taking responsibility again?'

She stopped and turned to him and although the words, when they came, were gravely spoken, the smile still danced in her eyes.

'I think I could accept it as the action of a concerned host,' she told him. 'Good thing I'm used to drinking cold coffee.'

Had that sounded casual enough? Paige wondered as she preceded him back to the dining room.

And why had she been so upset when she'd realised he had an ulterior motive in inviting her to accompany Lucia to Italy?

Because her stupid heart had fallen in love with the man, and love offers up any number of impossible scenarios where dreams *can* come true. But they *are* dreams, she reminded herself—doomed to that moment of waking when the magic lingers for an instant, before being lost in the reality of everyday life.

'Y-yes, thank you,' she stuttered when she realised

Marco was offering her fresh coffee before passing her a basket of warm, crusty rolls.

For a moment she was tempted to let the dream return, to imagine them as husband and wife, sharing a breakfast of coffee and rolls, at ease with each other, not tense and tetchy, their bodies perhaps filled with the warmth and satisfaction of the aftermath of lovemaking, one hunger satisfied, another tempting them to eat...

'Does a good fight before breakfast always make you hungry?'

Hungry? Had he heard her thoughts? Could she have spoken them aloud?

She looked up at Marco and then, puzzled by the amusement in his eyes, back down at her plate. She had four rolls lined up there, obviously selected by her fingers while her mind had been elsewhere.

'I was thinking of something else,' she said lamely, confused and embarrassed. She could hardly put three back when she'd already handled them.

'Keep them for the pigeons in the square,' he suggested, the laughter reaching his lips now, escaping in a low, incredibly sexy chuckle.

Stop thinking sex! she ordered herself. Think work.

'Why don't you think the service is working?' she asked, then frowned and added, 'Or should that be, why do you think the service is not working?'

'I take the point, whichever way it's phrased,' he told her, cupping his hands around his coffee cup as if to warm them and leaning towards her. 'But, if you don't mind, I would prefer you see it for yourself so you would not be swayed by my views.'

She grinned at him and said in tones of mocking wonder, 'Oh, do you think it possible people *could* be swayed by your views, Marco?'

'You are a tease, Paige Morgan. And, on top of that, a source of great annoyance to me. You have said that you are angry. Well, I, too, am angry. Paying for your own ticket was a foolish extravagance on your part.'

He didn't sound angry—more put out.

'Wounded pride, that's all you're feeling,' she retorted. 'I would probably have come to Europe even if Lucia's destiny hadn't dropped her in my lap, so I would have been paying my fare anyway.'

She'd watched him as she'd answered and both saw and sensed him biting back a cynical, 'First class?'

Just as well, for it would have started another argument—if only in defence of her own pride. Now she waited, because the conversational ball was in his court and she didn't want to argue about the travel arrangements again.

'Do you believe in destiny?'

The question was so unexpected, so far wide of the line she'd been following, she couldn't reply.

'I've never given it much thought,' Paige admitted eventually. 'I don't know if it's destiny as such which guides our lives or if we simply stumble along the path we happen to be on until something bobs up which forces us to take another track, or to detour and return later where the path is different. Then, from time to time, events erupt in our lives, making us hurry over bits which are rough, or linger longer where the track winds through nice grassy meadows.'

She could feel the heat of her own embarrassment climbing into her cheeks, couldn't look up and meet his eyes. How could she have babbled on like that?

She finished her coffee in one long draught, and pulled her handkerchief out of her pocket to wrap the bread rolls for the pigeons. The silence was growing heavier by the second.

'I suppose we should be talking about your service,' she muttered, anxious to lighten it—to clear the memory of her words from the air around them.

'Here,' Marco said, which wasn't really a reply so she had to look up from the impossible task of securing three rolls in her minuscule wrapping.

He was handing her his handkerchief, an immaculate square of white linen.

She took it, feeling more foolish by the minute, growing angry with him now for not answering her and so relieving the terrible tension.

'The public health system in Italy is always under strain so most businesses arrange private health cover for their employees.'

Release at last!

She sighed, stood up and shoved the now-wrapped rolls in her pocket, signalling she was ready to leave.

'So employees can be treated in private hospitals?'

'Exactly, but that is the easy part. The cover is also tied in with pension funds and other benefits, but in rural areas, because the family and the church have traditionally played the supportive and caring roles, such ancillary services like your meals-on-wheels and domiciliary care do not always exist.'

'Then how do you provide help for people where family support isn't available?' Damn, she was becoming interested now in spite of herself.

'That was our problem. It is all very well having the funds to provide these services to the workers who have retired or to their families, but who is to do the work where there are no generic organisations?'

'You set up something yourself?'

He shrugged.

'That is what we have tried. My father started the pension scheme but died before the use or uselessness of it became apparent. Our workforce was still young, made up in the most part of men and women from the village, but as the business grew and we had to import labour—'

'Import labour as in immigrants from other countries?' Paige asked, wondering if there were ethnic considerations to take into account.

He came around the table and stood beside her, smiling slightly as if amused by her sudden switch from prickly and defensive guest to interested professional. She could hardly explain it was a defence mechanism on her part— an attempt to wrest her mind from fairytales.

'No, but people from other regions of Italy, particularly in the south where unemployment is much higher. When these people came they needed housing. Spoleto is too far away, the old village already overcrowded because now there was employment in the area the young people were not moving away. So a new village grew around the factory, first houses for the workers, then shops, a school. There was a school in the old village as well, but it was cramped and dark so when the new school came along children from the old village also travelled to it and the edges of the new settlement and the old village became blurred.'

'Which school did you and your sisters attend?' Paige found herself asking, although it had no bearing on his story.

He smiled as if pleased she'd remembered his words, the glint in his eyes playing havoc with her resolution to stick with reality.

'The old village school. The factory was much smaller then, and most of the workers still lived here on the hill.

It was to provide employment for these local people when the farming ways declined that the factory was built.'

Paige understood, remembering his talk of the 'old' system where farmers leased their land from the big land-holders, paying rent with a portion of their crops. Like sharefarming at home.

'Then, as the factory workers earned more money—or perhaps realised they would have a regular income, which was something new for people raised on the land—they wanted more comfort.'

'So some entrepreneurial type saw an opportunity, bought up land and began to build smart, new houses for them?'

Marco scowled and she wondered if she'd inadvertently insulted him. Had his grandfather or father built the houses?

'Exactly,' he said crisply. 'Bought land cheap, closer to the factory, which seemed like a good idea to the workers at the time, they could walk to work—and built just as cheaply.'

No, not his father or grandfather! Marco was an honourable man for all he'd manipulated her visit to his home, and she couldn't conceive him being bred by rogues. But she could pursue the shoddy real-estate deal some other time.

'And now?'

He sighed and shook his head at her.

'I should have explained all this earlier,' he said, and she chuckled.

'Exactly my sentiments,' she reminded him, 'although I may have expressed them more heatedly.'

He smiled again and she felt her body relax, spun helplessly into the vortex of his charm.

But it wasn't charm he was wanting her to see—it was his problem. A fact which became only too obvious when he said, 'Let's continue this in the car.'

The route to the village was familiar to her now, so, although her eyes were on the scenery which never failed to fascinate her, she gave her attention to his words.

'Originally, villages grew with need—spreading in the easiest and most logical geographical direction. The church was always the centre point as the priest not only looked after the community's spiritual wellbeing but many of the practical aspects of its existence. People went to him for advice, for help, and, as you do in your service, he referred them on.'

'Does the new village have a church?'

He glanced at her as if pleased by her perception.

'Blind Freddy would have seen that coming,' she assured him, which led into a diversion over colloquial expressions before Paige brought them back on track.

'So the lack of a church meant a lack of a central focus?' she suggested.

'More than that because, although the men could walk to work, the women now had a much longer and uphill walk to the shops and the market, and the older women—mothers and mother-in-laws who would normally attend mass each day—found it increasingly hard to reach the church. Even the older men suffered because the bars and cafés were too far away.'

'So, did everyone move back to the old village?' Paige asked, interested in the logistics of the situation but unable to see where community health came in.

'Many did,' Marco answered, slowing down as they drove through the square, then speeding up again as the road wound lower until the old houses of the original village were all behind them. 'Times have changed and fewer young people are happy to remain in the home of their parents or parents-in-law, so the young families like to move into the new houses close to the factory. After all, the school is there for their children and observance of the sabbath is no longer so rigid, so not having a church close by does not bother them.'

'And as we've now passed through the old village, do I assume your service is based in the new village? Is that your problem?'

He sighed, then shot a quick glance her way and a smile which tempted her to think of fairytales again.

'We have regular buses which run between the two areas so it shouldn't be a problem,' he explained. 'But it's as if an "us and them" culture has sprung up in the area, and if a service is used by one group the other group will shun it.'

He swung the car to the right, leaving the main road and entering a tree-lined avenue which eventually opened onto playing fields.

'Look,' Marco said, disgust edging his voice. 'It's end of shift for about one hundred men and how many are there, playing soccer? Four!'

Paige laughed and shook her head.

'OK, you've got me,' she admitted. 'What's the connection between a health service which isn't working and only four men kicking a ball around a paddock?'

'Kicking a ball around a paddock? You laugh at a game which is practically sacred to our nation?'

His shocked accents made her laugh even more, drawing more fire.

'What is wrong with you?' he demanded.

'Oh, Marco,' she said, swiping happy tears from her eyes with the back of her hand. 'You should have heard yourself.'

He made a strangled noise, as if swallowing an oath, then smiled, reluctantly, himself.

'I suppose I see it as a symptom,' he explained. 'In other times, at end of shift all the men would have a game. Back then the factory's bus brought the workers down to the factory and took them back to the village, and the bus would wait because everyone knew that men coming off night duty would rest better after they had had some exercise. Our factory soccer team was one of the best in the area for many, many years.'

'I agree with the exercise idea because it's good for both their mental and physical health. But you said there's still a bus,' Paige protested. 'What I can't understand is how the split in the housing arrangements of the workers has affected the football games.'

'Now the bus is owned by a bus company which runs regular hours—by timetable. If the workers have a kick of the football they must wait two hours for the next service. Our bus was stopped because it was deemed to be against competitive trade practice, although it was free for the workers. You have this trade practice in Australia?'

He sounded so affronted that Paige had to curb an urge to laugh.

'We do indeed,' she assured him, 'and it's not all bad, but bureaucracy can be too cumbersome when it's dealing with individuals, which is why our health service was set up.'

'Exactly!' Marco exclaimed, his hand slapping the steering wheel in what seemed like triumph. 'I knew you would understand it all completely!'

Oh, yeah? Paige thought, totally bemused by what she was supposedly understanding.

And as for completely...

CHAPTER EIGHT

THEY drove on and Paige looked around her. The new houses, for all Marco's denigration of the workmanship, looked bright and cheerful, and not too unlike the ancient village ones to jar *her* sensibilities. Then he pulled off and parked in a bay of tarred area beside a tall, stolid-looking building which seemed to shriek public offices.

She remembered why she was here and glanced towards her host. Even if she didn't understand as completely as he thought she did, she may as well speak out about what struck her.

'If this is where your health service is located, that's a problem for a start,' she said.

'I'd begun to realise that,' he said gloomily. 'It doesn't look welcoming, like your house does.'

'Forget the welcoming and think practical. It has no ramp access.' Paige pointed out the obvious. 'It's not only older people who have trouble with steps but mothers of young families who are struggling with a pram or stroller and probably a toddler as well.'

He led her up the steps and pushed open a heavy glass door.

'Do I keep going?' she asked, wondering where advice ended and criticism began.

'Door no good?' he asked.

'It should be left open or changed to automatic and slide open. Same reason as the steps.'

'That is easily fixed,' he agreed, 'but I think it is more than steps and doors keeping people away.'

133

Inside the door was a wide foyer, with corridors leading off it to the right and left and a bank of lifts directly opposite the entrance. Signs in Italian evidently pointed to the various services to be found in the building.

'This way.' Marco indicated the passage to the right but Paige hesitated.

'I don't think this is the best way for me to see it,' she said. 'If your family was involved in setting it up, how many people will risk upsetting you by saying truthfully what they think is wrong?'

'Risk upsetting me? I have no power over their lives. You take this prince thing too literally. I am nothing special in this town.'

So his temper was as uncertain as her own still felt.

'Oh no?'

'Well, there is respect.'

'There's more than that,' she told him bluntly. 'Many of these people are dependent on your family's factory for their livelihood.'

'So they won't speak the truth? That's what you're saying?'

'It's what I'm assuming.' She stared at him, wondering how to convince him. 'What have you already done to try to solve it? Surely you've spoken with staff, with patients, perhaps had a meeting of all those involved?'

He nodded, then answered grudgingly. 'I have done those things and been told things were working as well as in any other service.'

'Yet you know that's not true.'

His fingers tangled in his hair, leaving it in slight—and very attractive—disarray, then he sighed and muttered, 'An old man, a former tenant of my father who was very close to our family, died in his home in the village. It was three days before his body was discovered.

That should not happen if a community service is working. Someone should have known he was to be alone at that time and seen to regular contact, but one party thought another would do it and he fell through the net we spoke of at your home.'

And you're carrying the blame for it, Paige thought, seeing real pain in his eyes.

'Let's get out of here,' she said. 'No, better still, is there someone in the consulting rooms who speaks enough English to understand me if I ask questions?'

'Lisette, the co-ordinator, speaks it well. She is French, but married to a local man.'

'Then how about you leave me with her for a few days while you go off and do your own thing?'

He smiled, and the combination of unruly hair and teasing lips made her heart throb.

'My own thing, as you call it, is here today. Today I am the doctor. But I understand what you are saying—that we should not be too closely connected. I will go in and send Lisette out to you.' The smile disappeared. 'Not that it will work,' he added gloomily. 'By now the entire village must know a foreigner is staying at my home, and the news has probably spread to this lower village as well. They will put two and two together.'

He sounded so put out that she patted his arm.

'Don't worry, I'll do more watching than questioning. And listening too,' she added, grinning at him, 'because I'm beginning to pick up on bits of conversation so be warned.'

'Ah, now I must watch my words,' he said gravely, then he smiled again, so warmly that Paige wondered if there was a hotel down here where she could stay while doing her 'research'. It was definitely time she got away from him—time she got her body back under control.

As he walked away from her, she studied him. Was it because he was so unlike anyone she'd ever known that she'd fallen under his spell? James, for all his stated belief in women working, had seen her job as demeaning— her work with less fortunate people as some kind of social disgrace. In Marco she sensed admiration, and for all his inbred sense of family responsibility he was the first to admit his sister made a better manager of the factory than he ever could.

She was still pondering the make-up of the man when a young woman appeared.

'Oh great!' she greeted Paige in idiomatic English. 'Another blonde in town. I'll stop being a nine-day wonder. I'm Lisette. Francesco sent me to rescue you.'

Paige introduced herself and shook Lisette's hand. She was used, now, to people outside the family addressing Marco by his given name—and pleased by the sense of privilege that he didn't insist she use it.

'He says you're here to take a look at how we run. Please, ask anything you like. I know the service should work better, but we're all at our wits' end, trying to work out how.'

'Nine-day wonder? Wits' end? You have to be English!'

Lisette smiled.

'I grew up just outside London,' she explained. 'My father was employed by IBM. He took a holiday job there when he was at university and somehow he stayed on, pausing only briefly to go home to France and persuade my mother she would like living in England. She never did, which is why they returned home some years ago.'

They had walked together down the corridor as she'd explained, and they now reached a door which Lisette pushed open.

Another difficult door for potential clients.

The waiting room could not have been more unlike the one at home. With horrible anatomical drawings and quit-smoking posters adorning all the walls, it shrieked medical surgery, not community service.

'Is this the only place you have where people can come to talk to you?' she asked Lisette.

'Awful, isn't it? This is Vitti, our receptionist.' Lisette rattled off an introduction, then explained, 'Her name's Vittoria but she hates it, hence Vitti. Now, I have this room on the left and the doctors' room is on the right. Come with me, and we can sit down while I explain things. As you see, there's no one waiting for my attention although Francesco has a patient at the moment and several booked in for later in the morning.'

'Does he come in every day?' Paige asked, although she should have been thinking of the service, not Marco. And hadn't he mentioned Terni in connection to his work?

Lisette looked shocked.

'Oh, no! He has to earn a proper living like the rest of us. He's a surgeon at a big hospital in Terni but he tries to do one morning a week here to keep up his general practice skills. We need a full-time doctor but each time we get one he leaves so usually we have locums. The present locum is an older man. You will meet him this afternoon.'

The locum business was another obvious problem, and one Paige understood. All too often, community health centres couldn't afford to pay the wages permanent doctors required. At home she managed with volunteers, but that was in a town large enough to have a good supply of general practitioners. From the way Marco had spoken, this was the only service in the two villages. Perhaps in Spoleto there'd be someone…

The phone rang and as Lisette fielded the call Paige let her mind wander.

'I have a visit to make. Do you want to remain here or come with me?' Lisette asked.

'Stay here,' Paige said promptly. 'If you don't mind. I'll sit out in the waiting room for a while and pretend to read a magazine, see if I can get a feel for things— have a think.'

Lisette seemed to understand, which was just as well because Paige couldn't have explained it any more clearly but, sitting in the waiting room, it did give her a feel for things. People came and went, shown by Vitti into the room Lisette had indicated was Marco's.

As far as she could see, this part of the service was entirely medically oriented, but she didn't want to jump to conclusions.

'Well?'

She was alone in the waiting room when Marco appeared in the doorway of his office, and looked expectantly at her.

'Oh, I've been here all of three hours and solved the whole thing,' she snapped at him, mainly because he'd upset her equilibrium, not to mention her pulse rate.

'Yes, of course, but that wasn't what I meant. I was wondering if you were ready for lunch.'

Ready for lunch when her stomach was doing somersaults—perhaps the result of no contact with him for a few hours.

'Not with a stranger,' she said firmly. 'I may not have come up with any solutions, but I do think that the less we see of each other around here the better if this crazy idea of yours is to have any chance of working.'

'You didn't seem to think it such a crazy idea earlier,' he grumbled. 'You yelled about not being asked properly, but you didn't mention crazy.'

'I did not yell,' Paige argued, but he ignored her injured dignity and smiled.

'Well, raged,' he amended, propping himself against the jamb. 'What will you do for lunch?'

'The same as the locals, I suppose. I'll go down to the porchetta stand and eat some delicious hot roasted pork in fresh crusty bread.'

His smile broadened.

'Ha, I knew you'd develop a taste for it.'

She remembered the first time she'd eaten it, the juice running over her fingers, probably dribbling down her chin. He'd laughed when she'd complained about the mess and had handed her a handkerchief, his fingers brushing hers in the exchange, warming bits of her which had been cold for too long.

She sighed and wondered if she was being silly not to eat with him today, denying herself the pleasure of his company.

No, said her head. Not in the circumstances. This 'job' has given you the perfect excuse to draw back and get your emotions under control.

'Then I will leave now to go down to Terni, but I've arranged for Lisette to phone Anna who will collect you when you are ready to go home.'

Ready to go home! The little phrase sneaked into her heart and she had to remind herself that his house was not her home.

'No need to bother Anna,' she said crisply. 'Lisette can show me where to catch the bus—it's better that way as I'll get the feel of the local transport. I can walk up to the house from the village.'

'You do not need to do that,' he argued, and she grinned at him, and knew from the flash of challenge in his eyes he'd remembered her teasing remarks about his overdeveloped sense of responsibility.

'No, I don't need to,' she agreed, 'but as the patients who visit the centre catch the bus, I will have to include the experience in my research.'

'So you win again!' he said, but he was smiling, accepting her decision even though it overrode his plans.

'Was it an argument?' she tempted, wanting to see that light in his eyes again.

'Isn't it always?' he responded, but so gravely that the fun went out of the conversation.

'I will see you at home later,' he said. Once again the phrase snagged in her heart, but her ears had caught another message. A hesitation? Why? Was he likely not to return home this evening? Any evening?

She realised how little she knew of him and that, in the week they'd spent together, he'd rarely mentioned his work.

'Do you always commute or do you stay in the city during the week?'

'I commute,' he said, so abruptly she wondered if that was a problem. For him? Or for someone else?

'OK, I'll see you later.'

She tried for lightness, but the thought of someone else—a female someone else, perhaps—had rattled her.

Marco remained where he was in the doorway, going neither in nor out, and again she sensed uncertainty. Not a word she'd have associated with his prince-ship before this! Did he not want to leave her to lunch alone?

But when he spoke any hope that his thoughts might be personal was dashed.

'I am grateful to you,' he said, then he shifted, came

through the door and walked towards her, holding out his hand. 'And I will see you this evening.'

She took the offered hand for she'd caught onto the European habit of handshaking, but even a 'habit' handshake with this man affected her body and sent her mind back to fantasy land.

Where it remained long after he'd departed.

'Come, we will lunch!'

Lisette's reappearance brought her out of her dream, and she followed her new acquaintance out of the building and down the road to the square at the centre of the 'new' village.

As they lingered over coffee, knowing the office was closed until three, Paige half listened to Lisette talk while another part of her mind absorbed the atmosphere. Yes, the square lacked the antiquity of many she'd sat in with Marco, but it was still a place where people congregated, talking, eating, laughing, drinking—arguing as well, if the raised voices were any indication.

'The new village works on this level,' she said to Lisette. 'The square has the right feel to it.'

Lisette nodded.

'Yes, the new village is growing into itself, developing its own traditions, but the division still exists. For instance, although the doctors' patients come from both villages, all the clients I have spoken with this morning were from here, not the old village, and that's one of the problems.'

'Transport?'

Lisette smiled. 'I wish! No, it's that the service is seen as ''theirs'' by the people in the old village, yet it is the elderly people in the old village who are most in need of services. I should know, I live there.'

They talked around the subject, straying from it into more personal conversation but usually returning to it.

'Is there accommodation I could rent down here?' Paige asked a little later—surprising herself almost as much as she'd shocked Lisette, if her expression was any guide.

'But you're a guest of the Albericis,' she objected. 'Why would you want to rent something down here?'

'I'm interested in your problem,' she said, although an honest answer would have been 'to get away from Marco' or 'I like this place, this area. I'd like to spend more time here, but without the distraction of his presence'.

Realising that what she *had* said wasn't quite enough, she added, 'I thought I might stay on for a while, but I don't want the Alberici family to feel obligated to keep me.'

Lisette lifted her hands in a 'well, I don't understand but it's your life' gesture, then replied, 'There's a guest house which supplies meals. Many of the single men who work at the factory have lodgings there. Or there are a number of apartment buildings and, given that so many people moved back to the old village, I'm sure you'd find an owner willing to let one on a short-term basis. I'll make some phone calls when we return to the office.'

'That's great!' Paige said, excitement building within her as she contemplated her immediate future. Perhaps she'd get a car, revisit some of the beautiful places Marco had taken her and explore some new ones on her own.

They returned early to the office, and by six that evening Paige had not only checked out several furnished apartments but had chosen one and signed a month's lease.

*   *   *

'You cannot do this,' Marco decreed, much later. He was standing in the doorway of her bedroom where she'd retired to pack, after telling his mother of her plans over a dinner which he'd missed—held up at work. He looked tired, but as attractive as ever, setting her hormones into their usual frenzy of delight.

'Of course I can,' she countered, the words more casual than she felt. 'I'd like to get the feel of living in a village and I can't do that from here. Also, I'm interested in your problem but, as I pointed out earlier, it's much better that I'm not too closely connected with your family. This way, the villagers will find it easier to accept that I was employed to accompany Lucia home, and am now staying on to learn something of the health service.'

'You weren't paid to accompany Lucia home.' He ground out the words as if the non-payment was another bone of contention—one he still found difficult to swallow.

'No, but the villagers don't know that. Now, don't argue, Marco, because I'm going, and, unless you want to play the heavy-handed head of the health service board and forbid me to visit it, I don't think you can stop me.'

'Do you delight in putting me in the wrong, Paige Morgan?' he growled. 'Does it satisfy some feminine instinct in you to be always throwing what you see as my position in my face?'

She was surprised by the emotion in his voice, and by how he saw her actions, but she didn't let it show, smiling at him and saying lightly, 'No, to both your questions, but perhaps you see it that way because you're not used to women standing up to you. You must admit, you run a household where a number of women do say ''yes, Marco'' more often than they argue.'

'The day my sister Paola says ''yes, Marco'' without

an argument, I'll be surprised. You've just seen less of her and more of Anna. And as for Lucia!' He threw up his hands in a gesture of despair. 'She might say "yes, Marco" but she then goes ahead and does exactly what she wants.'

He was arguing but his tone had softened, as it always did when he spoke of his family. And he seemed more relaxed about, even resigned to, her imminent departure from his house. Perhaps relieved?

As she was—in one way.

He said goodnight, not asking about the arrangements for her departure. Perhaps his mother had already told him that Aldo was to drive her, with her luggage, to the lower village in the morning.

Nor did he visit her new abode that first week, although Anna dropped in regularly, Paola called on her way home from the factory and Signora Alberici visited, bringing two potted plants to give the place a more homely look. Friday evening brought Lucia and Alex, dropping in on their way home for the weekend, but no Marco.

'He's probably sulking because you moved out,' Lucia stated after she'd enquired about her brother's reaction to the move. 'Didn't ask him first and let him arrange everything for you. Although why you'd want to leave the Casa for such a small apartment...'

Paige hid a smile. Marco might not consider himself a prince, but his little sister had 'princess' in her blood!

When she saw him at the health centre the following week he was polite but distant, and she was glad when Lisette suggested they do some home visits. Anything to keep away from him.

Which worked for one morning at the health centre, but not when he finally arrived on her doorstep, two days later, holding a bunch of yellow roses in one hand. Apart from shutting the door in his face, there was little she could do to avoid him.

'Are you going to ask me in? The flowers could do with some water. I bought them in Terni, so they'll probably start wilting shortly.'

'Flowers?' she repeated, still too shocked to get her act together.

'These things.' He waved the roses helpfully in her face. 'House-warming gift. That is traditional in Australia as well?'

Of course! A house-warming gift. Not flowers for her at all! Except they were, but not in the way her silly heart had hoped.

'Do come in,' she managed to mutter. 'And thank you for the flowers. I'm not sure the apartment runs to more vases, but there's a large jug that will do the trick.'

She turned away, letting him follow her into the one room which was living room and kitchen, then bedroom when she unfolded the bed from the settee. The usual squeal of protest from the large armchair told her he'd not only followed her in but had sat down as well. Was he preparing to stay?

'Well, what do you think?' she asked, when she'd unwrapped the roses, put them in a jug of water and placed them, in the centre of the her small table, beside the flowers Lucia had brought.

'A typical soulless apartment, but if you prefer it to remaining in my home...'

His shoulders lifted in an expressive shrug.

'Did you come here because you can't stir up a decent fight at your place?' Paige demanded. 'Or did you have some other reason?'

Another shrug, but different this time—slow enough

for her to notice fatigue in his face and the lethargy of the movement. He was tired and she wasn't helping matters, trying to provoke an argument.

'Have you eaten? I was about to have supper. Lazy Aussie pizza—tomato, olives, ham and cheese spread on bread then toasted. And you could have some Colli Perugini to wash it down. Alex presented me with a case of Umbrian wines.'

He didn't reply immediately, instead looking around once again, his gaze lingering on the potted plants, the bright floor rug which Paola had lent her. Would he recognise them, remember having seen the kitchen items, the hanging rack of assorted implements Mirelle had insisted she would need adorning his own kitchen wall?

'So, all the family has visited, bar me,' he said gravely. 'Do you always feed them?'

'If they come at mealtimes,' she said, trying for calm although her mind was squirming with questions about his presence, her body in revolt for different reasons. 'Are you staying?'

He looked up at that.

'Would you like me to?'

The question was so unexpected she couldn't answer, then she realised, like the flowers, it hadn't been meant as she'd first thought.

'You would always be welcome in my home,' she said, with formal politeness.

'Ah!' he responded, as if some other question had been answered, but he did stay, sitting opposite her at the small table, eating the simple meal she'd prepared, talking of the wine and other Umbrian wines which had won international acclaim. Of the standards now imposed to ensure quality, then later, as they sipped their coffee, of his work at the hospital.

'You enjoy surgery?' Paige asked. 'I did some work in Theatres during my training but knew it wasn't ever going to be something I could handle. Too impersonal somehow.'

'You found it impersonal yet for the time the patient is in the theatre his life is in your hands? And those of the anaesthetist?'

Marco was so close she could see the muscles moving in his jaw and cheek as he spoke, watch the way his lips formed words.

Form some yourself or he'll think you've gone to sleep! her brain warned.

'It wasn't the actual operation that was impersonal, although the patient isn't a whole person in a theatre—just a shrouded form with a hole revealing a carefully prepped piece of flesh. It's the before and after stuff. You don't get to know the patients as people.'

'And you do in general nursing on a ward?' he argued. 'In Australia, perhaps, but here in Italy our hospital bed numbers have been so reduced by cost-cutting and other expediencies that the beds barely get cold between patients. And the nursing staff, though excellent, are too busy to be providing much care beyond what is necessary.'

'It's the same at home,' she agreed. 'Not enough time for patient-nurse relationships to develop. Although there, the length of stay has been greatly reduced as well. I think the powers that be use the excuse that research has shown a patient recovers far more quickly in familiar surroundings.'

He nodded, his eyes alight as if was enjoying the conversation—or was about to shoot her down in flames.

'You are right, but also wrong.' Shoot her down in flames! 'Because it spoils your argument about personal and impersonal.' He smiled, lifted his glass towards her in a kind of salute, then asked, 'Is it for that reason, lack of patient-nurse relationship, you chose community nursing?'

'I suppose so,' she admitted. 'Or perhaps it chose me. My father became ill four years ago and I came home to nurse him. There wasn't enough to keep me occupied all the time so everything grew from there.'

He sipped his drink then set the glass back on the table.

'Ah!' he said, his gaze catching hers, holding it, making the air tangle in her lungs.

'Ah, what?' she asked, trying to behave as if her pulse rate were normal, not galloping so fast she thought he could probably see it beating in the hollow beneath her chin or throbbing at her temple.

'It explains your talk of paths through life and rough patches where you hurry past. You were very close to your father?'

'Very close,' Paige admitted, then determinedly changed the subject. 'But we've talked enough about other things. Didn't you call in to see how things were going at the centre—to ask me what I thought?'

His smile teased its way into her heart, doing nothing to steady her still-racing blood.

'No, I did not,' he replied. 'I came, belatedly I will admit, to see that you were comfortable. I was put out by you spurning my hospitality, but that does not excuse my neglect of you.'

Paige chuckled, aware of the effort it would have taken for him to apologise.

'Very handsomely put,' she said, wondering if she should have added 'do come again', although that would have placed her inner self in more jeopardy. She resisted the politeness, although it pleased her that he seemed at ease. And that the fatigue had given way to relaxation, so much so that when she suggested they move to more comfortable chairs he stood up and smiled.

'If I get any more comfortable I will fall asleep. I must go on home.' He held out his hand, and as she took it, shook it and released it as quickly as politeness would allow, he added, 'May I call again?'

She nodded, so discomfited by the words she hadn't said herself—or perhaps that fleeting touch of his skin, his warmth—she couldn't speak.

By the time she reached the door, she'd recovered sufficiently to say, 'Perhaps next time we should discuss the health service.'

'Do you think so?' he asked, and on that enigmatic note he left, walking away without a backward glance.

CHAPTER NINE

Marco did come again, calling in so often that Paige began to buy extra food, to cook for two instead of one. The formality they'd established on that first visit set the pattern. He would arrive, shrug off his suit coat, unknot his tie, roll up his sleeves then relax into her one comfortable chair, sometimes sipping a glass of wine from the bottle he now brought as his contribution to the meal. She would alternate between fussing in her 'kitchen'— the bench which held a sink and small electric stove— and sitting opposite him on the settee, her legs curled under her, pretending a relaxation she was far from feeling.

They would then move to the table which seemed to shrink in his presence, and Paige would watch his movements, note silly things like the way the silky, dark hairs lay flat against the lightly tanned skin on his forearms— tell herself she shouldn't while her eyes recorded every fleeting image of the man, her heart hoarding them against the time she wouldn't have him there in person.

Each time he left she told herself she wouldn't ask him in next time because the tension was too great while he was with her, the sense of loss when he departed even worse. Yet she listened for the bell to ring each evening, summoning her to the door.

Until the final week, when he didn't come on Monday, or on Tuesday. She saw him at the office on the Wednesday, but he was back to Prince Impersonal, nodding formally when she handed him a written account of her impressions of the service. So, when the bell rang on the Thursday, it was hard to believe it could be him, and when he invited her to eat with him at a bar in the square she became flustered, muttering about lamb—which she'd had in the small refrigerator for three days and which was now in the oven because she'd decided it *had* to be cooked whether the awaited guest turned up or not—and eventually inviting him to eat with her instead.

'I have no duty this weekend. Would you like to visit Rome?'

He asked the question as they sipped wine before dinner, and Paige, who'd been expecting more talk of the things they usually discussed—his work, the service, Lucia's health—took a moment to register what he'd said.

Rome! Would she like to visit Rome? With Marco?

Do birds fly? Fish swim? Babies cry?

'No, thank you,' she said politely, although her heart was breaking as she spoke the words. 'It's my last weekend here and I've so much to do.'

He nodded, as if it didn't matter to him—which it wouldn't, of course—and began to talk instead about the service, thanking her for the report, asking for recommendations.

'Don't run it from a building,' she told him. 'The more I've thought about it, the more obvious that becomes. OK, the doctor's there, but what you're trying to provide isn't medical. Leave him where he is—or, better still, shift him to somewhere accessible—but don't include him in the services you're offering.'

He studied her in silence for a moment, his eyes remote, then with a slight shake of his head he seemed to refocus.

'Well, truthfully speaking, he isn't part of the service,

but it seemed convenient to tie the two together as he could suggest to Lisette what was needed for the patients. And, if it's not based there, what do we do with Lisette? Are you saying dispense with her entirely?'

'That might have worked if the doctor was a permanent fixture and knew all the people who were on his list. But—'

'But that's another problem,' Marco admitted with a deep sigh.

'And not one easily solved, according to Lisette,' Paige agreed, then turned to what could be fixed. 'I'd make her more mobile. She already has a cellphone with voice mail on it so she's contactable wherever she is, but let her go to people rather than them come to her.'

'House calls? Isn't that an inefficient management of resources? And it isn't how you run your service.'

Paige sighed. OK, she was pleased to be talking work. It dulled—slightly—the tingling in her nerve endings caused by having Marco in the vicinity, and took her mind off things like never seeing him again.

'Our service is different. It's a drop-in place which is convenient to all the people it serves. That area once had streets of huge old houses which have now been turned into low-cost flats or rented rooms. Most of our clients are within walking distance. Here, you're trying to cover two separate geographical areas separated by a very steep and winding road with a bus service that never seems to fit into appointment times.'

'So you're saying put Lisette in a car and let her visit. It would never work. Italian people will always welcome visitors, but the women are embarrassed if they haven't finished their housework. They would be uncomfortable, not relaxed.'

Uncomfortable—how she felt when he was near. Yet

more alive than at any other time, her blood still singing in her veins.

'Lisette explained that to me, so we thought if she had two mornings a week in the upper village and two down here, then afternoons she can visit in either area and, theoretically, on the fifth day do book-work and follow-up calls. Although the service has been working American hours, as you call them, from nine to five, no one ever comes in the afternoon so there's no point in having her in an office after one.'

'Will this suggestion be so different to what is happening now?' His eyes scanned her face as if seeking an answer there, making her feel even more uncomfortable.

'I think it could be. For a start, you could make set days for different people. Down here she sees enough mothers and babies to have a separate baby clinic one morning a fortnight. On the alternate morning she can run other programmes which need regular attendance— quit smoking, weight loss, nutrition classes for those who are interested.'

'Nutrition classes in Italy?' Marco objected.

'McDonald's in Italy?' Paige countered. 'It's a world-wide problem, particularly in the younger families where fast food has become a way of life.'

She smiled at the disbelief in his face and said, 'Well, we can scrap the nutrition classes, but I'm sure you get the idea.'

'I suppose you are right,' he admitted, so grudgingly she wondered how to bring up her next suggestion. 'Go on.'

'Like nutrition classes, other things are changing in Italian society,' she began, treading very carefully this time. 'Lisette explained how important the family has always been, and how the care of the aged was usually undertaken by younger family members.'

He nodded gloomily and she wanted to reach across and pat his hand in sympathy because for his over-developed sense of responsibility must have made the decline of this tradition seem criminal.

'Now young people, particularly young women, move away to find work. They live apart from their parents and grandparents and that's where the holes appear in your net as both generations are affected. Some of the young ones are missing family support and some of the less able older people have no family to care for them. Lisette and I have talked about meals-on-wheels. Do you know the concept?'

Another nod.

'It's been tried in many parts of Italy—even the gov-ernment has given money to community groups for this purpose—but I don't see what good it can do.'

'It puts someone in touch with your more isolated vil-lagers on a daily basis—well, six days a week, we thought. The priest already has volunteers who visit housebound villagers on Sundays, but if the service can organise something for the other days, without making it look like an incursion into the older people's privacy, then that's another hole closed. The priest is very sup-portive. He's offered to lend the church facilities for meal preparation and has a number of men and women already rostered to cook and deliver them.'

'To the old village alone?' Marco sounded suspicious, not excited, but as Lisette had explained how quickly welfare services could break down Paige wasn't entirely surprised.

'No, to both villages. The doctor—and I think you'll have to find a way to get someone to stay permanently

in town because this locum business is half your problem—will refer people to Lisette, who'll check on any
special dietary needs then list them with the volunteers.
It can be done on a temporary basis for people just out
of hospital, say, or where the wife is ill, and on a permanent basis for those who are having trouble coping on
their own.'

'Hmm.'

The noncommittal sound stung Paige to anger.

'Well, that's a nice reaction to a lot of hard work and
thought. Lisette and I have spoken to dozens of people,
all of whom managed to sound a lot more excited than
''hmm''.'

He smiled, sending her heart into spasms of delight.

'I was hmm-ing over the doctor problem, not your
idea, which is great if we can keep it working. The problem is that the population isn't big enough to pay a doctor
the kind of money he expects to earn. Patients must be
listed with a doctor, but even if every inhabitant of both
villages listed locally the numbers don't add up to a lu-
crative practice.

'Did you know that Italy produces more doctors per
head of population than any other nation bar Cuba, of all
places? No? Well, it does, but the majority want to specialise, to work in places where promotion is possible
then move into private clinics, even build their own eventually.'

'And you don't? Didn't specialise? Aren't you working in a private clinic, owned, if I've understood correctly, by some family connection?'

He shrugged and raised his hands—resignedly, not defensively.

'I was interested in surgery,' he protested, but she
sensed his heart wasn't in it. Or his mind. It was as if

her words had awoken some sleeping worry which went deeper than keeping a doctor in the village.

Not that his worries were any concern of hers. She talked on, telling him about the availability of the former schoolhouse in the old village where Lisette could hold her morning sessions, of the other rooms in the building, ideal for activities like a playgroup or a drop-in centre where older people could meet, play cards, be entertained, possibly cared for in a form of day respite for their regular carers.

'Once they sat in the square and talked and argued, played their games there,' Marco told her, his indignation at the changing ways barely hidden.

'A lot still do,' she reminded him, put out that he was meeting each idea with doubt. 'But it's hardly a peaceful meeting place these days with traffic zooming through, the bus coughing out exhaust fumes, kids on mopeds weaving in and out of the café tables and groups of youths "hanging out".'

He gave another shrug, and a nod of what she took to be agreement.

'You don't have to be so excited about it!' Paige snapped. 'If you want things the way they were, then leave it at that. These are only suggestions, which, I might remind you, you asked me to offer.'

She snatched the plates off the table, realised he'd left half the meal she'd cooked—the beautiful Castelvecchio lamb—and felt more aggrieved, slamming the dirty dishes onto the bench and controlling an urge to yell at him.

Then his hands rested on her shoulders, very lightly, but any touch of his could hold her motionless.

'I am sorry,' he said, his voice deep and warm. 'You have done so much for me, for all my family, and I treat you in this way. It is not your ideas which trouble me, Paige, but a personal problem which I must eventually resolve.'

His fingers tightened and he drew her back so she rested against his body.

'Two personal problems, in fact.'

The words were breathed against her hair and she thought she felt his lips move against it, felt the warmth of his breath on her neck. She shivered at the contact, and his hands slid down to her upper arms, brushed up and down as if to warm her, his touch so gentle it made her want to cry. Or turn and face him, let his lips touch her mouth instead of her hair, feel the kiss she longed for in every atom in her body.

But deep down she was aware that such behaviour would shock him—that, for all his worldliness, this prince's attitudes were moulded by the past when gentlemen took responsibility for their actions. They might also have taken mistresses but both sides had known the rules, respected the boundaries.

Not that she was mistress material anyway! She knew herself well enough to know that 'happy ever after' was the ending she wanted in her fairy story.

'You won't change your mind? Come to Roma with me?'

He used the Italian pronunciation this time, making it sound so much more seductive, and she wondered if she was wrong about his moral views. She hesitated, tempted. Should she throw caution to the winds and go away with him? Experience the magic of the fabled Italian city with the man she loved? Wasn't that what life was all about? Living for the moment? Seizing whatever happiness was on offer?

'No,' she said, answering him, not her tempting

thoughts. 'Lucia and Alex are coming for the weekend to say goodbye, and your mother is planning a big lunch on Sunday. I couldn't disappoint them.'

His grip tightened on her arm, his fingers no longer caressing.

'But you could disappoint me?' he demanded, and she knew she had to face him. She moved with difficulty as her body had been comfortable against his. Now she had to shrug off his hands and turn in the confined space so that he was very close, his mouth within kissing distance, his eyes asking questions she couldn't understand.

'Would I, Marco?' she asked, and heard the quavering note of hope in her feeble words. Tried again. 'Does it disappoint you?'

'Of course,' he said gruffly, then the unthinkable happened as his head tilted downwards and those lips, which she'd watched and had wondered about how they'd taste, closed in on hers, touching them gently at first, then with a growing pressure until she stood helpless beneath the onslaught of a single kiss, her body fired to flashpoint by its power.

At the time it seemed to last an hour, perhaps a day— a week—but later, when he'd gone, she knew it had probably been less than a minute before he'd lifted his head, looked into her eyes and said, with what had seemed like grave sincerity, 'Will you marry me?'

'W-will I what?' she'd stuttered, certain that the effects of the kiss had had severe repercussions in her brain.

He hadn't responded immediately, stepping back a pace and looking even more confused than she'd felt— if that had been possible. Then he'd ducked his head in a funny kind of gesture and had said stiffly, 'Marry me! Stay on in Italy. Here. Help Lisette sort out the service.'

Her arms had flown upwards in the gesture of utter disbelief she'd seen so often since arriving in Italy.

'Oh, don't be so ridiculous, Marco,' she stormed. 'Even your princely principles couldn't dictate that you have to marry every girl you kiss! And if you consider trying to sort out your villagers' health service is an enticement, forget it. I can do that at home!'

A harsh laugh escaped the tightness in her throat. She'd been asked the one question most women in love would have given their front teeth and possible an ear or eyebrow to hear, and she'd said no! Was she going mad? Was she the 'ridiculous' one, to want love from marriage, not an offer of employment? 'Oh, why don't you go home? Get out of here. Take yourself and your stupid questions somewhere else.'

She waved her hands at him, as if to see him on his way, but was surprised when he shrugged one shoulder, hesitated only fractionally longer, then spun on his heel and marched towards her door, an effect which was spoiled when he had to return to retrieve his jacket.

'I shall see you at the family lunch on Sunday,' he said, turning as he reached the door a second time. But he didn't offer his hand in farewell, and nor did she move to offer hers. She stood where he'd left her, watching him walk away, her heart already asking why she was so angry.

And why she'd been so quick to say no?

He was affronted, that's what he was. Marco tasted the English word he'd never used before, rolling it around on his tongue. She'd treated his proposal as an insult! Worse than that, a joke! Yes, she'd laughed! At him! A man whom many women would feel honoured to be married to.

No, that didn't sound correctly put. Now his English was deserting him! He steered the car up the winding road, a jumble of thoughts in his head, some mocking his own folly at coming out with a proposal in such an inept fashion, others congratulating him on a narrow escape, memories of his grandparents' unhappiness still vivid in his mind for love had not been enough to satisfy his nonna, her love of her home always gnawing at her spirit, making her restless and difficult then bitter, until, even when she'd returned to England, she'd been unhappy.

But that didn't excuse Paige. She did not know about his nonna—well, no more than bare details given as the reason all the family spoke English. She'd said no as if he didn't matter to her, yet could she be so appealing to his body and her body not be equally responsive to his? It was his experience that such strong physical attractions were usually mutual.

And beyond the physical was the fact that they were friends. Hadn't he established that with his visits to her apartment? And hadn't she acknowledged it by welcoming him in?

He felt an ache of longing in his body and knew he shouldn't have kissed her, shouldn't have started something he'd had no intention of finishing—even if she had been willing.

Or perhaps that was the problem? Perhaps he should have used more physical means to show his feelings for her?

He reminded himself that he'd held back because he'd wanted her to know his feelings went deeper than a physical attraction, then laughed aloud at such nonsense. He'd fought the physical attraction with every fibre of his being because he believed a match between them was not possible.

Tonight he'd lost the fight and, having kissed her, wanted more, wanted it to last for ever, if truth be told, hence his, as she had said, 'ridiculous' proposal!

He groaned and stopped the car at the bottom of the steps leading up to the wide terrace, remembered walking with her there the morning she'd arrived, captivated by her delight at the beauty of the view. Since then they'd walked the terrace often, usually after dinner, the scent of roses from his mother's garden weaving magic through the air, the gentle, blonde-haired woman weaving spells within his heart.

It wouldn't have worked, Marco reminded himself, climbing wearily out of the car and trudging up the steps, the music of the spring mocking him with its careless watery notes, the moon a travesty of a symbol of a romance that never was.

Now the time to move had finally arrived, Paige found she no longer wanted to travel in Europe, or even see Rome. When Marco walked out the door she shut her mind on Italy, phoned the airline and asked about flights home.

'Monday,' the English-speaking operator told her. 'We could offer you a first-class seat on Monday.'

Privilege for those who could afford to pay for it, she thought cynically as she confirmed she'd travel on that day and took the details of the flight, a late one, giving her time to travel down to Rome on Monday morning. No need to tell the Albericis she was going home. They knew she was leaving and would probably ask about her plans, but if she said Rome then waved her hands vaguely in the air they'd accept she was still undecided—probably offer innumerable suggestions about what not to miss.

Which is what happened. Anna, Paola and the signora

all talked of their favourite places, the husbands chiming in, only Marco not offering suggestions.

But he'd made his—two, in fact—and she'd said no to both. He was gravely attentive, punctiliously polite—and as distant as Antarctica! In contrast, she had gone the other way, almost Gallic in her excitement, her speech and gestures, revealing her fondness for this family who had welcomed her to their home but making it plain she was equally excited to be moving on.

Huh!

The very thought of leaving the two villages filled her with pain, while the knowledge she would never see Marco again made her insides clutch in helpless agony. Pathetic! That's what she was! But at least she could still pretend.

Marco drove her home, much later, when twilight was settling over the mountains and the valley was thrown into their shadows, the fields a darker green, the poppies already washed from sight by night's approach.

'My family has grown very fond of you,' he said as they approached the lower village and he turned the car towards her temporary abode. 'They will miss you. They also find it hard to understand your independence, refusing even to accept a lift on the first stage of your journey. How will you travel?'

He sounded put out—offended—and she touched him lightly on the arm—perhaps for her sake, too.

'Lisette's husband is driving me to Terni when he goes to work,' she began, and realised she was adding insult to injury that she'd accepted Benito's offer when Marco would have done the same. 'From there I'll get a coach. I'll be all right—my Italian has come on enormously since I've been here. I've always had an ear for languages.'

What a stupid conversation to be having with a man you loved and would never see again.

He stopped the car but made no move to get out—and nor did she.

'I want to thank you for all the suggestions you made about the service. I know Lisette is keen to implement them, although she is more a hands-on nurse than an organiser.'

'I enjoyed doing it, and hope it helps.'

Stupid or not, it was best to keep talking.

'As you refused to take a consultancy fee, I have donated money to your service back at home as I know it is dear to your heart.'

'You've d-done what?' she stammered, then knew she didn't want to hear it again. 'No, don't repeat it. I heard the words, I just can't believe them. Is it not possible in Italy to do something because one wants to—without hope of monetary reward? It's like your medical situation here in the two villages. You say no doctor will take the post because he or she will not make a fortune. Doesn't job satisfaction count for something? Wouldn't living in a place like this—with clean air, smiling, friendly people and such rich spectacular natural beauty—be worth more than money to the right man?'

She flung open the car door and stepped out, bending over to look back at him.

'Don't bother to get out. Princely manners are all very well, but there's more to life than good manners, Marco Alberici. It's been—interesting, I guess about sums it up! Goodbye.'

She slammed the door with a satisfying thud, then strode across the pavement and into the foyer of her building, angry with him yet furious with herself for letting him get to her.

Not that he didn't do it all the time—one way or another. Particularly since the day he'd made that abrupt, unloverlike proposal.

Paige went to bed, but couldn't sleep, haunted by the feeling that she was running away, leaving too much unresolved. Yet her heart told her she couldn't stay.

On the beautiful drive to Terni she answered Benito's questions mechanically, her mind on the village, the family, wondering about Lucia's baby, which she'd never see.

'You don't seem very happy to be leaving,' Benito said when she'd answered '*no*' instead of '*si*' once too often.

'Well, I'm not. It's a beautiful place and everyone has been so kind to me, but I can hardly stay there for ever.'

'Lisette is,' he reminded her. 'She is proof a foreigner can be accepted. She has grown to love the villages as much as I do.'

'I know,' Paige told him sadly. 'But she has you.'

Benito seemed to accept this statement as an argument-clincher and didn't mention her departure again, which was just as well because the closer they got to Terni the weepier she felt. So unsettled, in fact, that when he dropped her at the *capolinea* she went off the idea of taking a coach to Rome then working out how to get to the airport from there, and splurged, hiring a car and driver to take her directly to the airport.

Once through the departure proceedings and on the plane she allowed herself to relax. As it rose above the Eternal City she felt tears prick behind her eyelids.

I'll come some other time, she promised herself. When I've been home, settled down, got over Marco. Brave words when in her heart she knew she would never get over Marco.

Then why had she said no?

The question kept recurring although she knew the answer.

He should have whispered 'Ti amo'. Or more correctly, according to Lisette who had included love in every language lesson, 'Ti voglio bene'. But, no, it wasn't love which had prompted that strange proposal, just some outdated sense of chivalry—or a desire to see his precious health service running more smoothly!

She put her head back against the cushioned headrest, glad there was no passenger beside her, and tried to sleep. She ate when food was pressed on her by attentive hostesses, drank a glass of wine—Italian—determined not to think of Marco. Flying through the night in a metal capsule, high above the turning world, her sadness flew with her, an unwanted fellow passenger.

At Singapore she obediently left the plane, walking in the file of passengers to a transit lounge where they would sit and wait while minions of the airline dusted and vacuumed, refilled food trolleys and fuel tanks. Beyond the windows of the transit lounge the sun struck against the brightness of bougainvillea and purple orchids, but the colours seemed lurid and over-bright after fields of green with poppies scattered through them.

Having nothing better to do, she turned towards a row of seats set in front of a television screen. The commercial was in a language she didn't understand. Chinese? Singaporean? Did Singapore have its own language? Someone switched channels and she saw pictures of tilted houses, panic and disarray, heard words in English—Umbria, Spoleto, and the names of villages to the north.

In 1997 an earthquake had struck in Umbria, badly damaging the town of Assisi as well as many mountain villages. Again and again she'd seen pictures of the devastation, tilted houses, panic and disarray.

The thought carried her across the concourse to the airline's desk and she heard herself saying, 'I must go back to Italy.' She pushed her ticket across the counter with her boarding pass and a gold American Express card. 'Please, I must go back as soon as possible. Can you arrange it? Or someone else? Who should I see?'

CHAPTER TEN

It was another thirty hours before Paige was back at Rome airport, where she once again employed a credit card to hire a car and driver, this time to take her directly to the village, wondering if her credit would stretch this far and how she'd pay for everything if the projected sale of her house to the community service fell through.

Not far beyond Terni, the driver told her, the valley roads were blocked to all but emergency traffic, but by the time they reached that city they'd become friendly enough for the driver to offer to find someone who could help her.

'Finding someone usually requires money,' she told him. 'I don't have much in lira—or notes of any kind.'

'You are a nurse, willing to help in the emergency. No one would dare take money from you when you make such an offer.'

Paige smiled at his indignation. Even in the welfare system, it was common practice for 'presents' to be offered—why would helping earthquake victims be different? But apparently it was, and she was the winner for he managed to get her as far as Spoleto, then, within an hour, she was on the move again, this time in the high front seat of a water tanker, trundling along the road towards the mountain villages which had been shaken by the earth tremors.

On the way she learned that the area around the factory had been hardest hit, the new village all but destroyed.

'The gods have spared the old village,' her driver told

her—or that was what she guessed he'd said, his English being worse than her Italian.

Had they spared Marco and his family? It was the question which had filled her head since Singapore, becoming more insistent when she'd learned the quake had indeed been centred around the one part of Italy she knew well.

'*Fabbrica—pouf!*' the man said, waving his hand towards the pile of rubble which had been the Albericis' business. She didn't need a translation to know what he was telling her, and her heart jittered at the thought of what might lie ahead.

She remembered the mothers and young babies of the lower village she'd seen in Lisette's office. Had they escaped? Been saved? The limo driver had told her the estimate of deaths was forty-seven, including those still missing.

Let Marco not be one of them, let him have been elsewhere.

At six thirty-two on a Tuesday morning?

Like so many people, he'd have been in bed, or just up, preparing for a working day. Definitely at home and unaware of the terrible danger about to strike.

The truck coughed its way into the square and Paige shut her eyes then opened them again. The streets leading off the square had disappeared, filled with rubble from houses which had collapsed. *Carabinieri* and soldiers patrolled, guns slung across their shoulders or hanging from their hips. Three ambulances stood in a row across a cleared space at the far end, and beyond them she could see people moving.

She thanked the man and left the truck, heading for the line of ambulances, wanting to do something, anything, to help. Excited voices yelled to each other, hope, not despair, in the tones. Paige found herself praying that another person had been found alive, the toll reduced by one, death cheated.

Now she was closer she saw men digging furiously, ahead of them handlers with dogs and people with probes moving cautiously, poking into the piles of bricks and mortar, seeking the softness of a human body.

Were heat-seeking devices being used? She assumed they would be. Everything was called into play in such emergencies—and the Italian people were among the best in the world at handling these natural disasters.

Stopping by the most forward of the ambulances, she waited, her legs wanting to carry her further up the hill— to the old village and Marco's house—but her professionalism reminding her she might be needed here. After a rescue operation which was into its third day, most of those helping would be tired, would perhaps appreciate a fresh pair of hands.

'*Tre!*'

Three alive?

She moved closer, found a man wearing a white armband with a red cross on it—internationally recognised— and introduced herself, explaining that she was a nurse and would like to help.

Her Italian must have sounded good to him for he rattled off a reply, or explanation, but at that moment the first limp body—a child's—was lifted from the mess of twisted wreckage and passed gently from hand to hand along a line of waiting men and women.

'*Vivo!*'

Alive! The word everyone wanted to hear. There were muted shouts of joy, the digging more determined now as one child recovered gave them hope. Paige took the space blanket from the driver and wrapped it around the small boy, then another woollen blanket on top of it, for comfort as much as anything else.

'I will hold him for you,' she said in her halting Italian. The man seemed to understand, seemed pleased the child would have the warmth of a body against him instead of a cold stretcher.

She sat on the ground behind an ambulance and cuddled the frail form, brushing dust from his face and then holding him more tightly as a medic inserted a catheter into the boy's arm, started a drip and taped the needle in place. He handed the bag of liquid to Paige who realised she would be acting as a drip-stand as well as a provider of warmth. Already there were shouts signalling that another person had been dug out so she was glad she was there to be with the boy, to murmur soothing Italian endearments to him, calling him brave and precious.

Then the commotion beyond the ambulance told her that yet another person had been rescued, and this time a huge shout went up, as if those who'd toiled were savouring their victory over nature. People milled about— that particular cave of safety must have been emptied now for rescuers were getting food and coffee from a van, stretching, talking and laughing, relaxing a little as they waited for the dogs or men with probes to call them into action again.

She held the boy closer. When the two other victims had been stabilised, no doubt all three would be ferried down the valley to Spoleto, or even Terni. Then she'd have to find something else to do to keep her mind off Marco.

'What are you doing here? This is a restricted area. There is danger of more movement, aftershocks, a second quake. *In nom di Dio*, at least I thought *you* were safe.'

It was hard not to think of Marco when he was there,

towering over her and roaring at her, swearing in Italian and throwing his arms about. Then his emphasis on the word 'you' clicked in her head and she stretched her free hand towards him.

'Oh, Marco, your family? Were they hurt? Not…?'

She couldn't say the word, bit it back as memories of the Alberici family's kindness brought tears to her eyes.

'No, they are all right, but you must go. Aftershocks are still occurring, could go on for days more.'

He was kneeling beside her now and she could see exhaustion in the dusty greyness of his skin, could see the blood on his hands where he'd torn his skin, digging through the tangled bricks and steel and concrete with the other villagers in the desperate search for survivors.

She took his right hand, the one she'd shaken so formally so often, in hers and lifted it to her lips, kissing the wounds, the blood.

'I had to know you were alive,' she said simply. 'I couldn't go on living until I knew.'

He said nothing and she knew it had been a mistake to reveal so much, so she tried for lightness as she added, 'And, apart from that, I'm a nurse. Extra medical personnel are usually welcome at these times. See, I can hold a child until the ambulance is ready to take him.'

She took her eyes off the child long enough to check Marco's face, to see if there was any reaction to her words.

Big mistake, that! His eyes were burning into hers, ablaze with something she couldn't read but which made her heart flutter wildly.

'You had to know I was alive, Paige? You came back because of me?'

So he hadn't fallen for the 'nurses needed in emergen-

cies' routine—and why should he when the first explanation was the truer truth?

'Yes,' she said, then met his gaze once again.

'Why, Paige?' he asked, the blue of his eyes making
his skin look even paler.

She looked around her, saw the damage, felt the pain
it represented, thought fleetingly of life—and death—and
knew only the truth would suffice at this moment.

'Because I love you,' she said, her voice almost lost
in a new clamour further along the mounds of rubble.
Another body located—perhaps alive.

'But you said no when I asked you to marry me,' he
argued crossly, 'and now I must go and dig again before
you can explain such irrational behaviour.'

'Well, go!' she muttered at him, fearing for him as she
knew he'd put himself in danger. Angry with herself because she didn't want him taking risks she knew he might
have to take. 'And saying no was no more irrational than
you asking me the way you did. As if I meant nothing
to you at all! Like it was another example of your politeness to a stranger—another way to repay some imagined obligation!'

'Meant nothing to me?' He echoed her words in
amazement, but another shout brought him to his feet,
looking indecisive—which was very unlike the Marco
she knew.

'I have to go now, Paige,' he added sternly. 'Please,
accompany the ambulance to Spoleto and wait there. My
family is at the Hotel Gattepone. They will find a bed
for you.'

Having issued his orders in his usual princely fashion,
he departed, but Paige had no intention of leaving.
Having seen Marco's wounds, it had given her an idea.
She'd get a first-aid kit from one of the ambulances, and

would tend the rescue workers' minor injuries as they took coffee- or meal-breaks. In any situation where water and sewerage services had been disrupted there was a grave danger of infection. It wasn't much of a contribution but it was something, and it would give her an excuse to remain close to Marco.

She asked for and was given what she'd need, but when she saw her first patient she added sutures to the list. Fortunately her patient spoke enough English to understand that if she didn't stitch the jagged tear he'd sustained, lifting bedsprings off one of those rescued, it could become infected and not be able to be stitched for a week.

She cleaned the wound and hurried to the closest ambulance, asking for sutures, using her hands to mime what she needed and getting a large pack of supplies in return. The driver walked across to where she'd set up her makeshift clinic and watched her work, and she wondered about the training of ancillary personnel, something she'd never asked either Marco or Lisette about.

'You do this kind of work?' she asked him, putting the Italian words carefully together yet knowing they'd probably end up in the wrong order.

He held up his hands in horror, shook his head and mimed driving. Which, she decided, was fair enough. As far as she was concerned, driving an ambulance through Italian traffic would require more skill and training than nursing.

Three men came in with burns on their hands and arms, reddened skin with blisters yet to form but which, she guessed, would be classed as bad first degree rather than second-degree injuries. In a halting mix of English and Italian, she discovered they were the results of a flash fire when a small pocket of gas from a leaking LP tank had exploded close to them.

Gas! Explosions!

Her stomach churned uneasily as she imagined a larger pocket of gas exploding—pictured Marco somewhere near it and closed her mind against the thought.

None of the men were willing to go to hospital and, lacking any medication she could confidently use, Paige wrapped the wounds in dry, sterile dressings and let them return to work. If infection occurred it could be handled later—at the moment these men were too intent on their rescue mission to be feeling much pain.

Word must have filtered through the rescuers that she was there for them, and by the time dusk threw its shadows over the square she'd treated innumerable cuts, gashes, burns and sprains, set a dislocated shoulder back in place and sent that volunteer home with his arm in a sling. She'd even dressed a leg wound on a dog someone had found, buried beneath his dead master in the ruins of his former home.

The dog lay beside her, his head on her foot, as she wrapped up all her rubbish, taking care with used suture and hypodermic needles, winding discarded packaging around them.

The activity had moved further from the square and she could see lights being set up and the hear the roar of electric generators kicking into life.

A bus arrived bearing a new load of rescue workers, Lisette's husband among them.

'You've come back? To help us?'

He kissed her on both cheeks then hugged her warmly just as Marco reappeared, the glower on his face suggesting he wasn't nearly as pleased to see her as Benito had been.

'Come,' he said abruptly. 'You have done enough for one day. Tiredness makes for carelessness. We will return to Spoleto, eat, sleep, then I will come back for tomorrow's early morning shift.'

His eyes dared her to argue, but the effects of the long flights, the changes of time zones, the despair and worry were beginning to take effect. Tiredness was pressing on her, as heavy as a wet blanket around her shoulders, and she knew he was right. She needed sleep.

She knelt down and lifted the dog into her arms.

'I can't leave him here,' she said defensively, when Marco frowned and shook his head.

The frown cleared almost immediately, replaced by a soft smile.

'No, of course you can't, any more than you could have not taken Lucia into your home.' He reached out as if to take the dog from her but the animal snarled and snapped at him, so instead he put his arm around Paige's shoulders, steering her across the square and down the road leading into it, eventually turning off to where cars where parked in a grassy field.

'Where were you when you heard about the quake?'

They'd driven in silence for ten minutes, Paige remembering that stupid confession she'd made hours earlier, realising how embarrassing it must have been for him, thinking how awkward it had made things between them.

When he asked the question she was so relieved to be able to talk of other things that she answered without conscious thought.

'Singapore. I was in the transit lounge and saw a news report on the television. I remembered the pictures we saw at Assisi—'

'Singapore? You were going home?'

Uh-oh!

'It seemed like a good idea at the time,' she mumbled limply, scratching behind the dog's ears, pretending an indifference she was far from feeling.

'I thought you intended to travel once you were over here. You said you'd considered spending time in Europe while you weren't working, even if Lucia hadn't crashed into your life.'

'Well, I changed my mind!'

He glanced her way, frowning fiercely as if he couldn't comprehend the language. Then he flung up one hand and said, 'I cannot understand the English!'

'I'm not English, I'm Australian,' she retorted. 'And there's nothing to understand.'

'No?'

This time he was smiling as he looked at her—a teasing smile which made her body think all manner of things she'd forbidden it to think.

'You went home because of love,' he accused, 'which does and does not make sense to me because already I had proposed to you.'

'Which meant nothing,' Paige fumed. 'Not a single thing, without some indication of your feelings. For heaven's sake, Marco, we'd been together for what? Six weeks, on and off. For the last three of them you'd called in nearly every evening and the closest we'd got to personal contact was a goodnight handshake. Even Benito greets me more warmly than that.'

'I saw Benito greet you,' he said stiffly. 'He is too familiar by far.'

If she hadn't been so confused she'd have laughed, but fortunately she didn't because it seemed his pride was already suffering.

'You were my guest as well as my responsibility—and I know you hate that word, but it is how I was brought up to act. I could not take advantage of such a situation by pressing kisses on you or furthering my suit. And as well as that, there is another matter which has been concerning me—'

'Furthering your suit? Oh, really, Marco, would you say that in Italian?'

She *was* laughing now, but more from nervousness than mirth. Did he mean what she thought he meant?

There'd still been no mention of love. And what other matter? Perhaps she'd let that dangling sentence pass and continue her attack on solid ground.

'And what's more, you followed up your proposal by mentioning the health service. It sounded as if you were offering me a job, not...'

Love? She couldn't bring herself to say the word again. Wondered if he would.

Silence stretched between them, so palpable that even the dog must have felt it for he began to whimper.

'This is nonsense, all of it, but it is not the time or place to talk of this, any more than when I asked that question was the right time. It evaded me, slipped out or up, whichever.' Marco slapped his hand against the wheel, his confusion showing in his, for once, less than impeccable English. 'There is your home, of which you are so fond, your country, so far away... My grandparents... The medical situation...' Again his hand rose and fell in frustration but this time the dog took exception and growled again. 'And now the dog! No doubt if I so much as lay a hand on you he will sink his teeth into my flesh.'

'Oh, I'm sure he would,' Paige agreed, smiling as the ridiculousness of the situation struck her. Though what her house or his grandparents or some unknown medical situation had to do with anything she didn't know.

'It is not funny,' Marco told her, guiding the car carefully through the winding streets of Spoleto towards the top and the modern hotel where they'd had lunch on her first visit to the town.

'No, I suppose not,' she agreed, confused herself by the emotion vibrating between them in the car and explanations she couldn't understand.

He stopped in the square by the *rocca*, the ancient fortified castle which dominated the town, his fingers tapping impatiently against the steering wheel.

'I am too tired to think,' he admitted. 'To say the things I wish to say. And now we must go into the hotel where once again, without a doubt, my family will take you over, and will fuss and be all around the place.'

He sounded so aggrieved that Paige forgot her own tension and smiled again.

'Come,' she said gently, resting her hand on his arm. 'Right now, you need a hot bath, a meal and a good night's sleep. We can talk when the crisis is over, when we know for certain there's no one still buried in that rubble.'

He turned towards her, eyed the dog warily, then placed his hand on top of hers.

'Sensible Paige Morgan!' he murmured so gently, so softly, that in her ears it sounded almost like a declaration of love.

Not that 'almost' was enough but it would do for now!

She let go of the dog to open the car door, then took back her hand from Marco's arm so she could lift the injured animal as she stood up, but before she could move Marco spoke again.

'You will not run away from me again? Before we have time to talk?' he asked. 'Disappear when I return to the new village in the morning?'

'Like Cinderella from the ball? No, Marco, I'll be here.' She grinned at him. 'In fact, I'll be down there with you—or not far away. Even you have to admit I was quite useful.'

She saw his chin tilt into its determined pose and the lips thin in disapproval, and she touched his arm again.

'Wasn't I?'

He heard the smile in her voice, saw it dancing around her lovely lips and groaned aloud. If it hurt this much to contemplate her back down in the village—in possible danger—how much more would it pain him to *know* she was there?

'If I asked you not to go?'

The words sounded harsher than he'd intended and he saw her flinch—just slightly—then she turned to him and those gold-flecked eyes looked deep into his.

'But you wouldn't ask it of me,' she said calmly, not challenging him but stating a fact—leaving him no option but to agree.

Well, not to agree but to say nothing, which was just as bad as agreeing.

She moved, clambering awkwardly out of the car with the dog in her arms and, exactly as he'd predicted, his family closed in.

Well, Lucia closed in, racing across the parking area with scant regard for her condition and flinging her arms around Paige and the dog.

Which didn't growl at *her*!

He climbed out stiffly himself and locked the car doors, then crossed to the hotel steps where Lucia was now holding the dog while talking nonstop to both the animal and Paige alternately.

'I will take the dog home for the hotel will not like it,' she announced as Marco drew near. 'I would also like

Paige to come and stay with me, but she says she will be leaving early and needs a lift with you so perhaps she's best staying here, although I don't know if there are any more rooms available.'

His sister's eyes lit up and she smiled mischievously at him.

'She might have to share with you,' she added.

Just as he'd guessed. Already the family was taking over.

'She can share with Mamma,' he said repressively, but repressive had never worked on Lucia and all she did was smirk and make silly disbelieving noises at him.

'Well, I must go, for Alex will be home soon and will be worrying if I am not there. I will see you tomorrow, Paige, for I will be having dinner here at the hotel. I will tell you how the dog is then.'

Then she moved towards Marco, stood on tiptoe and kissed him on the cheek.

'Ciao, Marco mia,' she whispered, her lips pressed against his skin.

It was Lucia's usual farewell, but tonight it irritated him for she was still smiling in a silly way, as if she knew things he didn't.

'She's totally impossible!' he grumbled as he watched her walk lightly away from them, the dog cradled in her arms.

'But very lovable,' Paige added, and a hint of sadness in her voice drew him closer to her. Close enough to put an arm around her shoulders and draw her body against his, feeling her suppleness, her strength and warmth.

'As you are, Paige,' he said, wondering why exhaustion hadn't alleviated the sexual responses of his body to this woman. 'I—'

'Paige, you have come back to us!'

'I'll talk to you later—or tomorrow—or in a week, when all of this is over,' he muttered as his mother bore down on them, her arms outstretched in welcome to the woman by his side. 'Promise me you'll stay!'

She looked gravely him in the eyes, stood on tiptoe and kissed him gently on the cheek.

'I'm not going anywhere,' she promised, then turned to greet his mother.

Who acted exactly as he'd predicted, sweeping Paige off to her room, talking about luggage and finding clothes for her to wear, leaving him to find his own room, to shower away the dirt and tiredness, then, just for a few minutes, to rest on that soft wide bed...

'The hotel staff are run off their feet with all the extra people packed into their rooms so I brought you breakfast.' Paige's voice, piercing fogs of sleep, penetrating the blankness—probably a dream.

'Just rolls and coffee, but plenty of both,' the dream voice continued, then a slight movement of the mattress suggested she might be real, and he forced his eyes open and peered blearily into the gloom.

'Paige?'

'None other, and complete with breakfast,' she said, smiling brightly and sounding so nervous he had to look again to make sure it was her.

Paige Morgan nervous?

'I'll be right back,' he mumbled, hauling at the sheet to cover his nakedness and escaping to the bathroom where he tried desperately to get his head back in working order, piecing together what he remembered of the previous day.

Including her return!

And the reason for it!

He showered quickly, singing under his breath, ten feet

tall—at least. Then he remembered all the other problems and shrank back to normal size.

'I wish you to know I am going to give up being a surgeon and return to be the doctor in the village,' he announced as, with a towel knotted around his waist, he finally emerged.

Paige frowned as if she didn't understand what he was saying. Or didn't like what she was hearing! He hoped it was the first and explained further.

'To do away with locums, to be there and advise while they rebuild the village, to be a general practitioner not a surgeon.'

'Out of a sense of responsibility, Marco, or because it's what you really want to do?'

'What kind of question is that?' he demanded, thrown by the fact that neither of his surmises had been right.

'A sensible one,' she said. 'Is it a decision you have made with your head, or with your heart since devastation struck the village? If you take on the job for the wrong reason, it won't work. You'll be unhappy and the villagers will sense it.'

He scowled at her.

'I have been thinking of it for a long time. In fact, I was ready to make the move before I travelled to Australia.'

'And travelling to Australia changed your mind?' she prompted.

He threw his arms up in the air, remembered the towel, and brought them back down very quickly.

'You are being deliberately obtuse, Paige Morgan. I have told you of the problem with keeping doctors, but if I must spell it out then you should know it will make a difference to my income,' he muttered, 'especially now the factory has been destroyed and all family money must go into its rebuilding. I will be able to provide for you in comfort, of course, but not as well as I would have hoped.'

Now she smiled at him, eyes sparkling with mischief.

'Is this proposal number two? Or is your stiff-necked pride preventing you from asking me now you won't be able to drape furs and diamonds over me? Do you want me to say I'd as soon marry a pauper as a prince?'

She was teasing him again, but gently, and he remembered her words of love as she'd sat in the ruins of the square, holding a boy she did not know in her arms. More than anything, whether they married or not, he wanted her to know his feelings for her.

What to say? And how to say it?

'I love you, Paige Morgan. Will you marry me, Marco, neither prince nor pauper but myself?' He'd blurted the words out. No class at all!

He saw her smile, the sheen of tears in her eyes, and fell apart inside, unable to control a rush of physical desire so strong he had to clench his fists and press his fingernails into his palms to stop himself from seizing her in his arms and frightening her with his ardour.

He wanted her to answer his question, not respond to the physical attraction. Wanted her mind and heart, as well as her body.

The silence clawed at his skin, so bad he had to break it. He pretended he was far calmer than he felt. Tried for lightness in his voice.

'Did you bring enough breakfast for us both? Shall we share and make plans so when all this chaos in the villages is over we shall know the direction of our future?'

She chuckled and he felt the physical reaction kick in again.

No time for that now.

'Well?' he demanded, coming closer but not too close.

But still she didn't reply.

'It is your turn to say something,' he growled, as the indecision gnawed at his heart. 'To say, "Yes, Marco, I will marry you." Then after that we will work out all the details and talk about your house and the love you have for your home country and how we shall resolve it.'

'All over one continental breakfast?' she teased, her lovely eyes gleaming so brightly he realised he needed more cover than a towel.

He grabbed clean clothes from the cupboard where some hotel person had placed them and headed back to the bathroom, reappearing minutes later to find Paige had opened the curtains and set the tray on a small table in front of the windows.

A much better position than near the bed from his point of view.

'I am still not doing this well,' he complained, moving towards her, seeing the way her hair moved like the swish of a curtain as she turned from the view to face him.

'You're not doing too badly,' she assured him.

'Then why are you laughing?' he demanded. 'I can see the laughter in your eyes.'

'Oh, Marco,' she said, smiling through the words. 'Come, sit down, have some coffee and a roll, relax.'

He flung his arms into the air and muttered a short prayer.

Relax?

When his body was on fire with wanting her, his mind in chaos with so much unresolved between them, and people waiting in the village to be rescued?

'I'm not going anywhere—except down to the village with you. We've the rest of our lives to sort things out.'

'The rest of our lives? You mean that? Are you saying what I think you're saying? Ah, Paige!'

He reached out and took her hands, drawing her into his arms and clasping her against his body—desire giving way to a flood of emotion so strong he thought it might burst out through his skin.

'*Ti amo,*' he whispered. 'Aren't those the two Italian words all foreigners can understand? I could say it in a thousand ways, in a dozen different languages, and none could express the way I feel about you. You are my light, my sun and moon and stars. My love!'

Paige let the words filter into her consciousness, accepting them but even happier to finally be in Marco's arms, held in their strength, protected and cherished. She felt him move and lifted her head, met his lips as they descended and welcomed the heat of their physical attraction.

'*Dio Madonna!* This must stop,' Marco whispered an eternity later.

'Yes,' Paige agreed, pushing herself firmly out of those entrapping arms. 'You have responsibilities!'

She spoke gravely but he must have seen the smile trying to escape, for he put out a hand to cuff at her. She caught it in hers and they moved together again, knowing they must hurry, that they were needed in the village, yet unable to tear themselves apart just yet.

In the end it was breakfast that suffered. Cups of coffee gulped down, the rolls spread with jam and taken in one of Marco's large handkerchiefs to be eaten, picnic-style, on the drive.

'About your house,' Marco said, as he twisted the car down towards the gate leading to the village road.

Paige shook her head and turned to face him.

'What is this obsession you have about my house? Do

you feel, in giving up your surgeon's job, you'll be stripped of your title and dispossessed? Utterly destitute? Are you marrying me for my house?'

She asked the question lightly, but inside a quiver of alarm was building. Not another James scenario!

But Marco glanced her way and smiled before he said, 'I am marrying you for love, Paige Morgan, and you must never forget that. But I am concerned you will be unhappy in my country—that your love for your house, your country, will draw you back there, away from me. It happened with my grandparents, who were unhappy in the extreme. I could not live with myself if I were to be the cause of such unhappiness for you.'

Paige was so relieved by this strange explanation that she laughed aloud, touching Marco's shoulder.

'Oh, Marco! If you must know, my house has just been sold—to the community service. Well, I'm presuming it's been sold—that's how I've been paying for all these flights around the world. Yes, I loved it, because I grew up there, but it's a building, nothing more than that, and now put to much better use than I could make of it.'

'And your country? You will pine for it?'

She hesitated, knowing she must answer truthfully but not knowing what the truth might be.

'I suppose I might get homesick from time to time, I don't know, but your countryside has already stolen its way into my heart and filled my soul with its beauty.' She paused, aware there was more—a final commitment to be made. 'And you, Marco, will be with me. Wherever you are will be my home.'

They drove into the field below the square of the lower village as she made this declaration, which was just as well as he stopped the car and kissed her soundly, only releasing her when the clamour of a car horn behind them forced him to move to a more suitable parking place.

She opened the car door but he was there to hold it for her as she alighted, reaching out to take her hand, to steady her or just to hold it.

'So, Paige Morgan,' he said, when they stood together in the square, about to part, she to tend the workers, he to join them. 'Will you be my wife?'

She grinned at him.

'Is that a title or a job description?'

He smiled, then bent his head and briefly touched her lips.

'It is a pledge,' he said gravely, 'of a shared life together.'

'No orders? No taking over of my life? No over-developed sense of responsibility?' Paige teased.

'Of course not,' Marco replied, then he frowned at her. 'I must go now, but you must promise me, Paige, you will not venture further from the square than the food canteen, or get yourself involved in anything that might be remotely dangerous.'

She shook her head, chuckling at his words.

'Go and rescue someone, Prince Alberici. We'll work out the sharing stuff later.'

MILLS & BOON®

MEDICAL ROMANCE™

A FAMILY TO CARE FOR by Judy Campbell

Dr Sally Jones isn't quite sure what she wants next, so the locum post at the general practice in the Scottish Highlands will give her time to decide. Finding widowed Dr Rob Mackay there is not altogether a pleasant surprise, because he'd walked out on her in the past. This Rob is more serious, and the father of toddler twin boys, yet he attracts her as strongly as ever…

POTENTIAL HUSBAND by Lucy Clark
A follow on to Potential Daddy

When rural GP Vicky Hansen first met orthopaedic surgeon Steven Pearce, she was deeply attracted, but resigned to him returning to the city—until she found he'd bought some of her family land to renovate the cottage there. Meanwhile, he says, he will be her lodger!

FOR JODIE'S SAKE by Maggie Kingsley

Widowed for two years, Kate Rendall wants to start afresh, and takes the job offered by widower Dr Ethan Flett to care for his fourteen year old daughter, Jodie. Kate is shocked by the instant attraction she feels for Ethan, which is mutual, but while Jodie might like Kate as a carer, would she accept her as a mother?

Available from 7th April 2000

Available at most branches of WH Smith, Tesco, Martins, Borders, Easons, Volume One/James Thin and most good paperback bookshops

0003/03a

MILLS & BOON®

∿ MEDICAL ROMANCE™

DEFINITELY DADDY by Alison Roberts

Going back to work was exciting and hard for Harriet McKinlay. It meant putting her adored almost three year old, Freddie, in nursery. But why did the spinal unit boss, Patrick Miller, dislike her? She didn't know that Paddy had saved her life when she gave birth, or that he had the wrong idea about her morals!

TENDER LOVING CARE by Jennifer Taylor
Dalverston General Hospital

Midwife Sarah Harris had devoted herself to work, but the arrival of Dr Niall Gillespie, as new head of the department, changed all that. Except that Niall held everyone at bay— could she break down the barriers he had so carefully erected?

ONCE A WISH by Carol Wood
The first of two books

Dr Alissa Leigh, widowed with a small daughter, has been working at the health centre for a while when Dr Max Darvill and his son arrive. But Max's ex-wife is still very visible, and despite the friendship of the two children, Alissa isn't convinced that Max is really free to love her...

Available from 7th April 2000

Available at most branches of WH Smith, Tesco, Martins, Borders, Easons, Volume One/James Thin and most good paperback bookshops

0003/03

4 BOOKS
AND A SURPRISE GIFT!

We would like to take this opportunity to thank you for reading this Mills & Boon® book by offering you the chance to take FOUR more specially selected titles from the Medical Romance™ series absolutely FREE! We're also making this offer to introduce you to the benefits of the Reader Service™—

    ★ FREE home delivery   ★ FREE gifts and competitions
    ★ FREE monthly Newsletter   ★ Exclusive Reader Service discounts
               ★ Books available before they're in the shops

Accepting these FREE books and gift places you under no obligation to buy; you may cancel at any time, even after receiving your free shipment. Simply complete your details below and return the entire page to the address below. *You don't even need a stamp!*

YES! Please send me 4 free Medical Romance books and a surprise gift. I understand that unless you hear from me, I will receive 6 superb new titles every month for just £2.40 each, postage and packing free. I am under no obligation to purchase any books and may cancel my subscription at any time. The free books and gift will be mine to keep in any case.

MOEC

Ms/Mrs/Miss/Mr ....Initials ....
BLOCK CAPITALS PLEASE

Surname ....

Address ....

....

....Postcode ....

Send this whole page to:
UK: FREEPOST CN81, Croydon, CR9 3WZ
EIRE: PO Box 4546, Kilcock, County Kildare (stamp required)

MILLS & BOON®

Makes Mother's Day special

For Mother's Day this year, why not spoil yourself with a gift from Mills & Boon®.

Enjoy three romance novels by three of your favourite authors and a FREE silver effect picture frame for only £6.99.

Pack includes:

Presents...™
One Night With His Wife by Lynne Graham

Enchanted™
The Faithful Bride by Rebecca Winters

TEMPTATION®
Everything About Him by Rita Clay Estrada

0002/91/MB1

Available from 18th February